ℛ

Prescription for Murder

by HANNAH LEES

Women Will Be Doctors

℞

Prescription for Murder

by HANNAH LEES

THE SUN DIAL PRESS

NEW YORK

For

PAUL R. REYNOLDS, JR.,

Worker of Wonders

$\mathcal{R}_x$

Prescription for Murder

I

"BE A good little girl, now, and let me do the worrying." The tall scholarly chief smiled behind his glasses and patted the shoulder of his difficult patient. His voice was cornstarch-pudding smooth.

Cyrus suppressed a snort. *A good little girl.* It would hardly have been his description of Miss Caroline Faine, directress of nurses at the City Hospital. The woman was pushing forty and pushing it hard, but maybe she still looked young to Willoughby. Maybe she even looked good.

His eyes rested callously on the face on the pillow, more interested momentarily in the full, rather cruel lines of her mouth than the drawn look around it that meant nausea, more interested in the arrogant arch of her nose and the domineering lift of her heavy eye-

3

brows than the furrows between them that meant pain. Probably she'd been a pretty toothsome morsel in her day, if you liked them feline and man-eating which Cyrus didn't, but that day was definitely past. And it would be hard to imagine her ever speaking to a man with anything but antagonism. She certainly hadn't just now. *Girl!* Willoughby didn't need to carry his diplomacy toward Training School Office that far.

Cyrus was feeling good and sore at the whole setup. There were plenty of other sick people in the hospital needing attention. And yet here he was; here was Willoughby, probably the most important internist on the staff; here was Dora Cutter, resident in charge of Nurses' Infirmary; here was Miss Markham, head nurse of the infirmary; and here were a few assorted blue nurses all gathered around one not particularly enticing, not even particularly instructive bed.

Hell, there were dozens of more interesting diabetics over on Medical, if diabetes was what you wanted to see. But simply because someone important in T.S.O. had gone on a chocolate-fudge binge or something . . . And you couldn't tell him she hadn't. These sex-starved women were always finding crazy outlets like that. If you couldn't get a man, have a fudge sundae, only if you were diabetic a man would be a lot safer.

"You say there have been no dietary indiscretions.

Quite sure of that, are you, my dear?" Cyrus' suppressed snort changed to an admiring grin. For all his stiff collars and silk handkerchiefs, for all his pudding smoothness, Willoughby never got left behind. It had been a little game with Cyrus since he came on Willoughby's service, three months ago, trying to outguess him, but it hadn't happened often.

"Really, Doctor, you can't pin the blame for these new symptoms on me." Cyrus glanced sideways at Willoughby to see if he was going to resent this open sneer. Apparently he wasn't. His face was as smooth as it always was, and the smile stayed on.

"I wouldn't dream of trying," he soothed, "but you realize there must be some reason behind them and we've pretty well ruled out the possibility of any infection."

"Well, you're the specialist, of course, but if you ask me, I haven't been getting enough insulin." The woman spoke with effort but her eyes as she raised them to the chief's face were bright with malice. And why the hell doesn't she take care of her own diabetes, Cyrus thought, and glanced at Willoughby again.

"It was enough till three days ago," he was reminding her gently. "If it suddenly isn't enough now we'll see that you get more." He was smiling down with the indulgent tender smile one would give a favorite child who was being difficult.

And this couldn't be just T.S.O. diplomacy, Cyrus

thought suddenly. This was damn funny. Of course he'd never seen Willoughby with a private patient before. On the ward he was pleasant, sometimes even flattering to the women patients, but he wouldn't take any nonsense. If this was just playing politics, it made you sick both on principle and because it meant you had the guy doped out all wrong, but it didn't seem quite like that. If it was just private-practice charm, the guy was nuts. He ought to know that what the woman needed was a good stiff kick where it would do the most good, but she wasn't getting it.

Now she was saying, "Of course a good many people have told me that Dr. de Grasse is particularly skillful in handling diabetes. I've always stood up for you, but . . ." And Willoughby was answering, still gently, "It's your privilege to call in de Grasse, if you like, my dear, but I think we'll have you straightened out in a few days." And Miss Faine was retorting, "Well, see what you can do. I can't bear the smell of Dr. de Grasse's pipe." And Willoughby was laughing easily, as if at a very funny joke.

Cyrus glanced at Dora Cutter to see if she shared his disgust. It was damn uncomfortable, seeing a big shot like Willoughby being psychologically pushed around by a lousy nurse. Even if she was head of T.S.O. she was still just a nurse, and Willoughby was—well, Lester Willoughby, not only the

6

acknowledged authority on diabetes in the city but almost certainly the next Professor of Medicine at the University, and incidentally quite a guy. Probably the Faine couldn't help it; probably she was so used to bullying the nurses it was second nature. And probably Willoughby was just too decent to resent it. But Cyrus wasn't; it made him boil.

If it made Dora Cutter boil she was concealing it well. The youngish woman doctor stood at attention with the athletic ease of an old hockey player. There was an inquisitive look in her candid brown eyes and just a ghost of a smile on her wide straight mouth, but it didn't tell anything. Be interesting to know how Cutter doped out a female like Faine, Cyrus thought, with what for him amounted to respect. She'd have some involved psychiatric theory that sounded screwy as hell, that would make everyone roar if she aired it, but it would probably stand up.

His eyes slipped past her to Miss Markham. The plump, fair little nurse had a disapproving expression on her round face, but whether it was disapproval of Miss Faine or Dr. Willoughby, or because one of the students had just rustled her uniform was hard to say. The students looked as if they were suppressing giggles. They often looked that way at these ritual gatherings, but Cyrus resented it all the same. He was glad when the doctors moved out into the hall leaving Miss Markham to tend to the patient, was glad to see the indulgent look drop from Willoughby's face.

"Now what was the last blood sugar, Harvey?"

"Four fifty, and CO_2 of thirty-two. Pretty definite acidosis, isn't it, sir?" Cyrus objected to sirring chiefs on principle. Cyrus objected to respect for anyone or anything that couldn't be tested and proved in black and white like a scientific experiment, but Willoughby had taken some pretty severe testing in his three months over Cyrus. He seemed to merit the sir more than most.

"Very definite," he was agreeing drily, and his forehead was wrinkled in concentration. "Yet the girl's been getting sixty units a day since Friday. It's puzzling. She called me because she felt dopey and was having headaches. Her blood sugar when we took it then was 225, a sudden jump from around 130. Of course diabetes does get suddenly and inexplicably more severe once in a while, but I've been watching this case of hers for the last eight years and it's gone just like clockwork. I can't help feeling there is something definite behind this new trouble, but"—he shrugged—"I haven't been able to find it."

"Could she have grown careless about taking her insulin, Dr. Willoughby?" Dora Cutter suggested deferentially. "Perhaps just because her case has been so well controlled for so long she forgot the insulin

8

several times and now won't admit it. Miss Faine is rather a strong-minded person."

Willoughby smiled, again with that ghost of tender indulgence. "It's quite true that if she had been careless she never would admit it, but for eight years she's been the most conscientious patient I've ever had." He smiled again. "Not that I'm entirely trusting. I considered that possibility. But her niece, the little student nurse on Children's, has been giving her the injections for the last forty-eight hours, since she has felt so unwell. I hardly think she could have been careless too. She's very devoted to her aunt, you know."

"I know." Dora Cutter frowned a little. "I've always wanted to make a study of Miss Moore." And I'll bet you have, Cyrus thought, grinning at the tall, raw-boned psychologist. Nothing would be more down her alley than the strangely withdrawn student who was the niece and almost constant attendant of this domineering diabetic.

Diabetic, his mind went back to the actual medical problem. A sudden increase in severity like this. There had to be some reason. Maybe if you ruled out fudge sundaes it wasn't such a dull case after all. Infection? But Willoughby had gone into that. Of course it did happen without your ever finding out what was behind it, happened sometimes with apparently nothing behind it. Well, probably not. **Probably** there was always a reason if you could find it.

"Could anything be wrong with the insulin, sir?" he suggested idly.

"Oh, scarcely. It's one of the accepted brands and they check them pretty carefully, you know. Still, a patient occasionally ceases to find some particular brand effective, so I've ordered a different one. We'll start that at once. I'd wash out her stomach too, I think, and give a little saline under the skin, and . . .

"Oh, good morning, Miss Moore." A slim figure in blue and white stripes was hesitating a few yards away. Her young face had an anxious look, but it was hard to tell how anxious because her fair hair was pulled back so tightly that it would have drawn her features into a worried expression even if she were feeling gay. When Dr. Willoughby spoke, she murmured, "Good morning, Doctor," in a low monotonous voice and put her hand nervously up to her cheek. And that's what Cutter would like to dig into, Cyrus thought. Wonder what she'd find.

He studied the girl curiously as she went on in the same monotone, "Miss Kenny said I was to special Aunt Caroline as long as she needs me." It was a screwy combination, this aunt and niece. Aunts and nieces weren't usually so devoted, and these two, Miss Faine with her domineering stares, the kid with eyes that nobody ever saw because she never looked directly at anyone . . .

Dr. Willoughby had put on his professional smile again for a moment. "It will be a great comfort to her to have you around, but I can't have you worrying, my child. Diabetes is always an unpredictable disease, but there is no reason why we shouldn't be able to standardize your aunt at a new dosage level in a short time. It would help us, by the way, if you could think of anything to throw light on her condition. No"—he raised his eyebrows in humorous interrogation—"no unusual parties?"

"No." The niece shook her head passively. "Aunt Caroline was very careful about her diet, always. She ate in her room, you know, from special trays. She never went to parties."

"And you know of no other change in her life or her habits?"

The student shook her head again. "No, unless . . ." She hesitated. "Could a sudden emotional strain have any effect, Dr. Willoughby, because . . ." Her monotonous voice had become momentarily more monotonous, as if she were choosing her words with care. "My aunt has been rather upset about something for the last week, something that has made her angry several times. Oh, something quite personal. I'm sure it isn't important," she added quickly, "only

I thought if it could have anything to do with her condition . . ."

"I scarcely think so." Willoughby dismissed the idea without curiosity. "I imagine this change of brand will bring her blood sugar down. Take care of that saline and lavage, Harvey, and keep me informed. I'll drop by this afternoon.

"Good-bye, Dr. Cutter." He nodded briefly to the woman resident. "Have no hesitation in suggesting anything that comes to your mind, to Harvey here." But his words were as perfunctory as his nod. Willoughby didn't like women doctors much. Nobody did. Cyrus wondered as he had a hundred times since he started medical school just what series of peculiar urges made them willing to buck all that prejudice and antagonism. Maybe some of them didn't know what they were getting into till too late, but Cutter must have. She'd been a psychologist before she studied medicine, and been psychoanalyzed into the bargain. She was only studying medicine so she could do analysis herself, which hadn't helped the prejudice much, though it probably helped her to rise above it. Cyrus glanced again at the resident's serene face.

Well, she didn't have to rise above his, not since that boy with the ulcers when she was on Medical with him a couple of months ago. He and Willoughby had given the kid the newest and most accepted medical treatment, but it hadn't touched the trouble. Nothing had till Dora Cutter had diagnosed the case as having an emotional background and gone ahead and cured it. Cured by psychotherapy right under their noses without one act that could be called interference either, and as tactfully as only a psychologist could, with nothing but a little intensive social service work. Willoughby might not have forgiven her for it, but Cyrus had. You couldn't hate anyone for out-thinking you. You were too busy being surprised.

"How about it, Emotional Angle?" He grinned when Willoughby had disappeared down the hall and the student into Miss Faine's room. "Think a bad temper tantrum could bring on acidosis? Say yes, and I'll have to believe it."

The young woman's ruddy face flushed at the compliment, but she shook her head. "I don't see how," she said seriously. "I should think excess emotionality would tend to burn up sugar rather than produce it. Besides"—she smiled a little bitterly—"if tempers were going to cause acidosis, I'm afraid Miss Faine's diabetes would have got out of control long before now. I've had two kids in bed here in the past month after sieges over minor breaches of discipline. I wouldn't call her an ideal directress of nurses. There's a real sadistic streak, I think . . ."

"Ideal wenches don't get to be directresses, Cutter. They marry or"—Cyrus grinned at her—"get to be

13

lady docs. You'd kind of like to know what that personal problem was, wouldn't you?"

"Yes." She smiled. "But if she's here long I'll probably find out. I wonder if it had anything to do with Evelyn. I don't think her aunt is very good for Evelyn."

"Privately, we don't think she's good for much of anything, do we?"

"Well," Dora laughed faintly, "she's good at maintaining discipline and getting a tremendous amount of work out of the students. What are a few nervous breakdowns in a cause like that? Anyway"—she laughed again, though not particularly gaily—"she makes my work as resident here more interesting. Four out of five ailments seem to have a nervous etiology, usually due to fear—or hate. Nice place we work."

"Lovely!" Cyrus shrugged. "Since this isn't a psychiatric case I suppose you're glad Willoughby has shoved all the dirty work on me. Of course being in the infirmary, this lavage and saline and all is technically your baby, and if you'd like . . ." He paused with burlesque deference.

"I wouldn't think of interfering, Doctor. Of course if I think of any valuable suggestions . . ." She laughed again and vanished into the ward.

Cyrus had got the grin off his face by the time he was inside the door of Miss Faine's room. Cutter was quite a gal. If all women doctors were like her, or all superintendents of nurses . . . He glanced at the figure in the bed. She was lying still, as if temporarily defeated by her illness, but her burning eyes stared angrily at him as if resenting the advantage he had of being on his feet while she was on her back. He looked away in discomfort and his eyes fell on the bottle of insulin on the bureau.

"This the new brand, Miss Moore?" He picked it up and glanced at the label, wondering why in the world one brand could be effective while another brand wasn't. They were both insulin. Oh, of course you read reports of that being true but it didn't make sense. "Better give her that thirty units right away and then order the trays for the lavage and the saline. I've got to get down to the ward and I want to make Miss Faine comfortable before I go." He spoke politely but most of his mind was on the insulin. There could be some defect in manufacture, of course.

"By the way," he added suddenly, "have you got that last bottle of insulin here?"

"Why, no." The student put her hand nervously up to her face. "Dr. Willoughby said she was obviously getting no effect from it, so I just left it in her room over in the Nurses' Home." There was alarm in her voice.

Pretty grim, Cyrus thought, to spend your life in

terror of doing something, practically anything wrong, and wondered how much Miss Faine was responsible for that. "Sure," he said, and gave her a warm disarming smile. "It wasn't any good to you, was it? Only if it should be defective or anything the company ought to know. I thought I'd have it tested if you'd find it for me."

He turned back to the bed and found the dark eyes of the patient fixed on him with a new malevolence. Now what the hell have I done or said, he wondered. But all he did was touch the skin of her face experimentally and say casually, "Pretty dry, aren't you, Miss Faine? Well, we'll fix that up with the hypodermoclysis."

II

"EVELYN, Evelyn, isn't it time for my insulin?"

"Not quite yet, Auntie."

"Evelyn, listen, if I still have to have a special nurse tonight I won't have anyone but you. I don't care if twenty-four-hour duty is against the hospital regulations. I'm directress and I can change them if I want. Do you hear me, Evelyn?"

"Yes, Auntie, of course I'll stay. I'll have a cot brought right into the room, dear. I want to be here with you."

"You didn't show it when you were gone all that time this morning, Evelyn. What were you doing then?"

"I was looking for the insulin that Dr. Harvey wanted. I can't find it. I'm sure I left it right on the

17

bureau. But I asked all the maids and they didn't know anything about it."

"They're always lying about things," said the directress impatiently. "It doesn't matter anyway. There was nothing wrong with that insulin. I just haven't been getting enough, that's all. See," she half raised herself up from the pillow. "I'm better already."

"Oh, be careful, Auntie." The thin anxious face of the student nurse contrasted oddly with the rugged dark features of the woman. It was as if they should have changed places, the student in the bed and the older woman watching over her. And when Miss Faine pulled herself upright and sat there panting from the effort and said, "I am careful, I'm always careful. I have to be, Evelyn. You need me. You've nobody else," it was almost as if they *had* changed places for a moment, particularly as the girl seemed to shrink a little smaller at the words.

"Oh, I do need you," she declared passionately. "I'd die without you. You must get well quickly, Aunt Caroline."

"I'm practically well now." The woman shot her niece a compelling glance. "That intern who was here, Evelyn, I saw him looking at you and smiling. You mustn't forget you're not like other girls. You mustn't forget it for a moment, you know. It would be terrible."

The girl seemed to shrink still more. "He didn't look at me," she whispered. "I kept my hand up to my face. And it wouldn't have mattered if he had. I didn't look at him. I never look at them." There was a hopeless note in her voice, but her aunt didn't seem to notice.

"Work, that's the important thing, work, and with it comes power. Power can make up to you for everything else, Evelyn. Nobody can take that away from you. But men, even if you were like other girls, they're animals, all of them, wild animals, Evelyn. You can handle them if you keep a firm hand and a distance. But never trust them. You can trust me, Evelyn, but never make the mistake of trusting anyone else."

"Dr. Willoughby," the girl said in a low voice, "he doesn't seem like an animal."

"Oh, Willoughby," the aunt's voice softened slightly but there was scorn in it. "He's more like a woman. You don't need to be afraid of Willoughby. He means well enough. But all the rest of them, and particularly that—that one I've told you about. If you ever see him coming, turn your head away, and if you have to speak, speak quickly and go on your way. He's not to be trusted, Evelyn. He might do anything."

"I know," the girl's voice was low and soothing. "You've had a lot to worry you lately, darling. Just stop thinking about it so that you can get well. Now it's time for your insulin." She picked the bottle up from the bureau and inserted the syringe.

"Why isn't it in the icebox? Insulin always ought to be in the icebox."

"Miss Markham said that since you were getting it so often I could keep it here and put it in the icebox at night. It means leaving you less often, dear." She filled the syringe carefully and slid the needle deftly into the woman's arm. "I'm so glad you're feeling better," she said in a dreamy voice. "I'm so glad you're feeling better."

But her mind wasn't on her words. They couldn't all be wild animals. They didn't all look like wild animals. That Dr. Harvey maybe, he was fierce and frightening, and most of the others, but not all. Her mind was back on the trip to her aunt's room an hour earlier. She couldn't help it that Dr. Bowman had caught up with her and walked along with her. There hadn't seemed any harm in it—he was so quiet and nice and you could hardly see his eyes behind his glasses. It wasn't her fault that he'd asked her to go to a concert with him. Of course she couldn't go, even if he was really as nice and kind as he seemed. But it was funny that he should have asked her. Nobody ever had before. Perhaps being a resident on Psycho, he didn't notice people being different so much. Perhaps . . .

20

But perhaps that other man had sent him to make trouble. No, better not even think about it. Aunt Caroline was right. Work was the thing, work and Aunt Caroline. "I'm so glad you're better," she repeated monotonously, soothingly.

III

OVER in the Children's Clinic the last mother and child had disappeared into the last examining room. Sally Pepper stacked the cards together to be sent over to Social Service for investigation, pushed her fair hair back from her forehead and stretched. It had been a long morning with a lot of headaches. Parents trying to chisel out of paying, children trying to scream their way out of being examined. Sometimes, she thought wearily, it almost seemed as if her father was right about it being absurd for girls to work so hard to give themselves the illusion of usefulness. Sometimes an afternoon of bridge and gossip looked terribly gay and glamorous. But that was only because you had forgotten what an afternoon of bridge and gossip was really like. And what was the

22

good of learning all that stuff about social trends and the necessary education of the masses if you weren't going to use it? She stretched harder. Less chance of being ploughed under, come the revolution, this way.

"Trying to dislocate a shoulder?" said a sardonic female voice.

"And be on the receiving end for a change? Heavenly thought." Sally looked up, her curly face curling further as she grinned. "Hello, Miss Kenny. How's the children's ward?"

"Screaming its head off." A small angular starched figure with a brown monkeyish face that sat incongruously under the pleated charm of the City Hospital cap was leaning on the desk. Her hair was crisply pepper and salt and her brown hands were bony. She'd been the head nurse on Children's for five years and swore she hated children, but had never quite convinced anyone. "You have one of those mornings too?"

"Sort of. I miss Evelyn Moore. She goes around like an astral body but she can handle kids. She's not sick, is she?"

"Her aunt is." Miss Kenny dropped into a chair as if her feet wouldn't hold her a moment longer and shook one of her Red Cross shoes reproachfully. "Every time I get a new pair they're half a size larger and they still hurt. There ought to be a complaint called Nurses' Feet. There is, as a matter of fact, though the orthopedists don't recognize it. Sometimes, after I've stood respectfully all day for that precious assortment of males we call chiefs, I . . ." She puffed her cheeks out in a disrespectful gesture. "Miss Faine's diabetes seems to have gone bad all of a sudden," she explained belatedly.

"Miss Faine? Why, I didn't know she had . . ."

"Most people didn't. Always said she ate in her room for a little peace and quiet. Lot of backbone that girl has. Guess I know her as well as anybody in the hospital except maybe Evelyn, the squirrel. We've been here together long enough."

"Evelyn's not really queer," defended Sally. "I often wonder"—she hesitated—"well, if she isn't too much under the influence of anyone as strong-minded as Miss Faine."

Kenny shrugged. "Bound to be under somebody's influence, a kid like that. Anyway, Miss Faine will be under her influence for awhile now. I gather she's pretty sick."

"What rotten luck! This happening just after she'd gone in as directress."

"Rotten, though as far as being directress goes, Miss Faine has been directress in everything but name for years. Some people are just made to run things, and she's one of them."

Sally thought of the brief glimpses she had had of the suppressed violence that was Miss Faine, and

24

shivered a little. It was hard to imagine her helpless in bed. "Well," she said as lightly as she could, "I hope Evelyn is doing the running for a change. It would do her good."

"Just a pair of lousy gossips. What would do who good?"

Sally looked up quickly at the deep voice and her creamy face got a little pink. For over a year now she'd been having run-ins with that voice. Several times she'd out and out accused its owner of being tough-skinned and too coldly scientific. Once, when she wanted to keep a kid in the hospital till she could get him away from his drunken father, Cyrus had said she was crazy. He'd said they needed the kid's bed, but the ward had become mysteriously quarantined with measles so the kid couldn't leave. She could still remember that episode. Probably the whole hospital could. Cy had taken plenty of a beating about it. Another time when she had been fighting a politician who wanted to get his child into the hospital free, Cyrus had sicked the newspapers onto her. It had offended her patrician desire for privacy and she had blown him up about it, but it had shamed the city politicians into a clean-up. The trouble was, his nickname Hard Boiled kept fooling you. And the trouble there was that the guy had worked to earn that nickname mostly to live down the nickname Humanitarian Harvey his father had had before him. Well, he'd never fool her again, the big cluck. She smiled up at him.

"Hello, Hard Boiled, come gossip too. We're talking about poor Miss Faine."

"Oh, he'd be too busy," Kenny said, "and this isn't your preserve, big shot. What is it, business or pleasure?"

"Philanthropy." Cyrus perched his long body on the edge of the desk and pulled out a crumpled pack of cigarettes. "Smoke, Kenny?" He waved them tantalizingly under her nose. "Go ahead, I'll only report you."

"Thanks, I never break regulations for anything less than a drink. Philanthropy? Don't know the word."

"Coming here every day to take a woman to lunch, Kenny, that's philanthropy."

"Only I never go," said Sally serenely. "I've heard that when an intern brings a woman into the dining room the other men all clap and stamp."

"That's only if they smell an engagement. You'd be perfectly safe with me."

"My mother will be glad to hear it." Sally pulled down her mouth. "But I'll take my corned-beef hash with the usual female society, thanks, chum. Ask me again."

"Sure, tomorrow. About Miss Faine, you're talking about one of my patients."

"Your patient?" Sally raised her eyebrows mockingly.

"Well, Willoughby's and therefore vicariously mine. Anybody whose stomach I've just washed out is a patient of mine, whether she likes it or not."

"Gosh!" Kenny looked up with concern. "Is she that bad?"

"Blood sugar 450, CO_2 of thirty-two is bad as I like to see. Damnedest thing, too. Kenny, there's not another thing we can find wrong with her. Little Willie thinks it's the brand of insulin she's been using, so we switched that this morning. The last blood sugar I took will tell the story. Want me to call and see?

"Hello," he picked up the phone without waiting for an answer. "Nurses' Infirmary. Miss Poole, please. Hello, hello, Harvey speaking. How's your patient? What? When? She has? That blood sugar come through yet? How much? No kidding. Swell. I'll call Willoughby."

He grinned around the phone. "Old right-again Willoughby. The blood sugar's way down. Getting more like herself, the kid said, said it in a weak voice too. Bet I know what that means."

"Everything short of the horsewhip," Kenny snorted.

"Thought she was a friend of yours."

"She is, but I like my friends with spirit." Kenny

was grinning. "I can handle 'em even when they get to be directresses. Guess I'll drop up this afternoon with a bedpan full of roses and tell her so. This place'd go to the dogs under Miss Wiley. That assistant's blood cells are floating in corn syrup instead of serum. Already she's given six nurses the week-end off because their boy friends are going to camp. Faine wouldn't stand any of that drivel. Faine knows where a man's place is."

"Where?" Sally encouraged her.

"Under the thumb or, even better, under the boot, with a slight grinding motion of the boot." Kenny rose, still grinning. "She's right too. You have to fight for your life in this totalitarian outfit."

"Everett's not my idea of a dictator," Cyrus caught her up.

"Well, he's not so bad." This amounted to eulogy from Kenny. "But the rest of the doctors around here wouldn't make life worth a nickel if we went soft over 'em. 'Bye, you two, but look out for this intern, Pepper. He's the kind of a guy who'd just as soon expose a whole ward to measles, remember."

"But only in a good cause." Sally smiled at Cyrus mockingly. "And he'd never let you prove it on him."

"That's quite a woman." Cyrus was looking after Kenny with a puzzled frown. "Hard as a brick wall and swell as they come."

"Wonder if she's really hard or if it's just protective coloring. . . ."

"Sure, she's hard; couldn't be friends with Faine if she wasn't."

"Maybe Miss Faine isn't really hard either. Maybe she was disappointed in love and it soured her."

"Love," Cyrus snorted. "You think everybody's soft inside because you are, Vassar. Some women wouldn't recognize love if it came up and kissed them. Kenny and Faine are two of those, and save your sympathy, they don't miss it. Only thing I can't figure is why a softie like Evelyn takes so much from a woman like Faine. Think she's just dumb?"

"She isn't dumb," defended Sally for the second time that day. "You ought to see her handling the kids down here. I'd like to know what's behind that funny gesture of hers, putting her hand up to her face as if she wanted to hide it."

Cyrus stared. "That's what Cutter said this morning." He shrugged. "You women are too analytical. Well, the kid's got a job of handling on her hands now, all right. I hope for her sake Miss Faine gets well fast. Though maybe I should hope for the hospital's that she doesn't." He grinned. "Life's too complex. Lunch? Food? Drink?"

"No, thanks."

"How about a movie tonight, then?" He put his hand in his pocket and pulled out a dollar bill and a few coins. "I'll come out to Whitbourne and take you to a nice cheap local one."

"All right." Her smile was suddenly wide. "Drive on out with me after work and have dinner first."

"Dinner? With your family?" he stared. "Why this sudden cordiality?"

"Mother wants to meet you. Oh, nothing personal. Only she's heard you're Dr. Harvey's son."

He scowled. "I knew there was a hitch. She used to know the Old Humanitarian?"

"She was a patient of his. Thinks you must be a very fine character." Sally's mouth twitched as she said what she knew amounted to an insult.

He scowled harder. It was all right to have inherited a guy's brain. It had been a good brain and nice to think you might have, but as for softness and belief in humanity that had kept an office packed and a bank book empty for most of a generation, as for having to take over a well-worn but apparently hardy tradition of general sweetness and light, the hell with that. Science was the thing that counted, that and facing facts. You didn't get a nickname like Hard Boiled, praise the Lord, by cooing over sickness and pain, and damned if you'd let any Whitbourne female coo over you and how much you looked like your illustrious father. Damned if you would. But mirrored in the back of his mind was the alternative —hospital pot roast. Maybe you could go and manage to duck the cooing. He looked wistful. "Is it going to be a good dinner?" he asked. "It would kind of have to be, under the circs."

"Roast beef, I think, and probably Yorkshire pudding," she said offhandedly. "Nothing very good but of course it's Monday night.'

The vision of the hospital pot roast became clearer and more revolting. He shrugged. "It's a date. That is, if my distinguished patient is doing all right, but I won't promise not to snarl occasionally. Call you this afternoon, huh?"

She watched his figure disappear through the door and then gathered her things together and set out for the social service dining room. It wasn't going to be very exciting. She wondered what Cyrus would do if next time he said "Lunch"? she said "Sure."

IV

"HELLO, hello." Cyrus' voice was as resentful as it was sleepy. Nobody, no matter who, had a right to drag a guy away from a dream of Yorkshire pudding served by a beautiful blonde, especially when the blonde and the Yorkshire pudding were both exactly the way they should be, soft underneath but crisp on the surface. As he struggled to make his arm reach out and pick up the receiver, he had been tasting the roast beef and Yorkshire pudding, so different from anything you ever got in the interns' dining room. He had been feeling Sally's hand in his own, so different from any hand he'd ever held before.

He was still feeling that hand as he said hello. It had been a dumb thing to do, holding her hand through the movie. Kid stuff, but that was just why

32

it had been so swell. Sally had the right approach to most things. She could hold a guy's hand and like it and know that it didn't mean a thing. Couldn't when a guy was only an intern and who the hell wanted it to. "Hello." Nobody had a right to snatch that hand away from his like this. "Hello, what's that? The devil you say." The hand was gone and he was awake with a bang. "When? How's she feeling? Oh, for Pete's sake! Don't worry, kid. I'll be right over."

He sat there on the edge of the bed groping for his trousers, cursing. You get a diabetic back on the road to normal by changing her brand of insulin. You get her blood sugar starting down and her spirits starting up. You leave her one evening feeling fine, drop in at midnight and find her asleep, and the next morning at six o'clock she's right back where she was twenty-four hours ago. Screwy? It was more than that; it was darn serious. No wonder the kid had sounded scared. Hell, he suddenly realized, as his hands found the white duck of his pants, so was he. Because there just wasn't any reason for it. The only thing that could make that happen was not getting any insulin, or getting enormous quantities of sugar. And she was getting insulin, lots of it. And however great her secret craving for chocolate creams might be, she wasn't well enough to go out and get them, even if she wanted to choose that way to commit suicide, which would be a singularly lousy one. And

Evelyn Moore wouldn't carry her subservience to her aunt that far, or you wouldn't think she would.

"Evelyn, go out and get me a pound of candy, dear, at once please."

"Yes, Auntie, as soon as you've had your insulin." He snickered unfeelingly at the picture. That was the bunk, of course, but there had to be something. Why, the woman had been well enough yesterday afternoon to have a whole roomful of company and enjoy it.

He could see her dark face when he had come in around two and found her sitting up in bed. He and Willoughby and Bliss Everett all in a body. Funny how embarrassed the superintendent had been when they overtook him in the hall leading to the infirmary wing, as if he'd been caught on his way to an illicit rendezvous. But then Everett wasn't the kind of guy that would be at ease in any female wing, and to have to go consult the directress of nurses on her sickbed because an intern had had a row with a nurse was a good deal for the superintendent of a hospital to swallow. Funny he had consulted her, as a matter of fact, except that you gathered Miss Faine had sort of got people in the habit of consulting her in the last six years. You still wouldn't think Everett would, and he'd been pretty funny, telling about it, hemming and hawing, and yet having to get it out so that Willoughby wouldn't think he was coming over just because of Miss Faine's bold black eyes.

And they sure were bold and black. The way they had gleamed when they all came in the door. She'd said a perfectly polite, "Good afternoon, Doctors"— but then she'd added, and there had been more triumph in her voice than apology—"I feel very guilty making all you busy doctors come to me this way. You must know how much I regret my indisposition." But she hadn't sounded regretful—nor very indisposed, either. She'd just sat there in an old scarlet bed jacket that would have made her look almost handsome if it could have covered up that hardness in her, and held court.

Kenny had come in and sent Evelyn away for a couple of hours rest, and Miss Faine had let her go. It was true friendship between those two, all right. Miss Faine being willing to let Kenny special her and Kenny being willing to give up her own afternoon relief to tend to a bad-tempered pal. Maybe she'd enjoyed the scene as much as he had, though. He had a picture of her moving quietly around, straightening bottles, arranging flowers. She hadn't brought roses after all and not in a bed pan. She'd brought a little vase of forget-me-nots, which was kind of out of character for Kenny but seemed to have pleased Miss Faine. People came in and out, Miss Markham, Miss Wiley, Dora Cutter, a half dozen or so other assorted nurses, and then of course Willoughby and Everett.

Oh, sure, she'd enjoyed it, and something to enjoy too, all those peope bustling around the bedside of one Miss Caroline Faine, who didn't mean a thing to nine hundred and ninety-nine people you'd meet on the street, and yet here in the hospital was a sort of queen bee, so important that the biggest chief on the medical staff came to see her twice a day even though she was getting better, so important that the superintendent of the hospital came to consult her on a minor matter of discipline. And so important that she made no bones about talking back to him either.

Cyrus wasn't supposed to know that, of course. Everett had stayed on for a bit after Dora Cutter took Willoughby and Cyrus into the ward to listen to a chest that sounded to her like pneumonia. It probably was pneumonia, too. But coming past Faine's room a few minutes later he had noticed the door was shut and Kenny talking to another nurse down the hall. Willoughby was going on theoretically about chests and maybe Cyrus hadn't been listening as carefully as he should, but as they passed the door he had heard voices, rather loud blurred voices and then Everett's voice clearly for a moment, "I tell you, Caroline, you can't do it." That was all. Apparently Willoughby hadn't heard, for he had never stopped talking. But it was pretty funny. She had probably been telling him off about her nurses' rights as opposed to the poor interns', and Everett wasn't having any domination today, thanks. There was satisfaction in that thought. Funny he should call her Caroline. Oh, maybe not so funny. She'd been around here for a good many years now.

Gosh, he thought as he hurried across the gray, dawn-lit court to the long building where all the wards were, where on the third floor at the very end the Nurses' Infirmary was, gosh, he was getting in a dumb enough state to think almost anything was funny, what with the crazy way this case was behaving. It wasn't his line imagining things, but he'd sure been doing it. Imagining unusual solicitude in Willoughby's manner to Miss Faine, imagining something sinister in a kid's nervous habit of holding her cheek—that had been Cutter, but it had got him noticing it too—imagining embarrassment in the way Everett behaved to Willoughby, and now trouble between Everett and Faine. Oh, the hell with imagining. If Miss Faine was as bad as the kid seemed to think, he had enough on his mind. What could be causing it anyway and what could you do except order still more insulin and keep up the salt and fluid intake?

Nothing apparently, and yet, when he saw the directress shaken with nausea and too dopey to have

37

any fight in her. when he felt the dryness of her skin, he was pretty sure that just insulin and more fluid weren't going to be enough. And he felt a sudden abstract rebellious anger. Diabetes was a controllable disease, by God. You could control it and you would. People didn't go off this way any more. Oh, they used to, fifteen, twenty years ago, before the discovery of insulin. You read about that and it wasn't very gay reading, but all that was past. Why, science had diebetes licked to a standstill.

Of course infection could upset the picture, any infection anywhere could upset the insulin requirement. His mind went back to the problem as he took blood to send to the lab for stat examination. But Willoughby had gone into that. Unless he'd somehow slipped up on something, the only other thing was diet.

"Listen, kid," he said softly out of the side of his mouth as he inserted the needle in the vein of the motionless woman in the bed. "I know we've asked before, but are you darn sure you aunt hasn't been eating anything beyond the trays from the diet kitchen, because . . ."

He could feel the arm jerking suddenly and looked down to find Miss Faine's eyes wide open in angry protest. "Idiot," her lips formed with difficulty. "Fool, I've got to live. Get to work and get me well."

38

"Hold your arm still, then. That's the first step," he ordered, and looked away from the uncomfortable intensity of her eyes to the student nurse standing across the bed.

"She hasn't eaten much of anything," she murmured in her flat voice, but there was fear in it now. "Not even all that was ordered for her. She wants so desperately to get well, she'd never do anything that might interfere." She caught her breath. "She seemed so much better last night, Doctor, and then toward morning I noticed she was sleeping almost too heavily, and then she suddenly began to complain of pain and nausea again and . . ." She looked down at her aunt and put her hand quickly to her cheek. "Tell me what to do," she whispered.

Cyrus looked away from her too. All this loose emotion. What the hell good did it do! It didn't make him any more anxious to lick this case. He was anxious enough as a simple scientific problem. Given a diabetic who suddenly gets worse, then suddenly gets better, then just as suddenly gets worse again, why, why, why? You wanted to think and all this emotion was just distracting.

"Give her fifty units of insulin right away," he said expressionlessly. "I'll start the saline and call Dr. Willoughby as soon as the blood sugar report comes through."

Willoughby, arriving shortly after eight, serious

but perfectly serene, brought some direction back to the case, even though by then Miss Faine was pretty close to coma. "Maybe we'll never find it, Harvey," he said thoughtfully, "but there must be some outside factor. I'm going over her again. If I don't find anything . . ." He examined the patient minutely, asking questions as he examined. Often the niece had to answer. Miss Faine was almost too weak to speak. Gall bladder? Tonsils? Sinus headaches? The questions and examination went on, and to everything the answer was no. After a quarter of an hour Willoughby shook his head. There was a baffled expression in his small shrewd gray eyes.

"There's no sense in trying protamine insulin at this point. It's slower acting than the unmodified and, besides, I tried to standardize her on that several years ago and she got frightful urticaria from it. The only other thing is crystalline. The newest thought seems to be that it works just as fast as regular and is sometimes a little more effective. Call the drug room, Harvey, will you, and have a bottle sent up at once.

"See who that is and tell them Miss Faine is too sick for visitors." There had been a not particularly timid knock on the door. Cyrus opened it.

"Oh, good morning, Dr. Everett," he said, standing back.

"Morning, Harvey. Hello, Les. How's your patient? I thought I'd just drop by and . . ." There was

40

that embarrassment again, but Willoughby cut short his explanations.

"We're having a good deal of trouble with the insulin dosage," he said, going to the doorway and talking in a low voice. "She's really in pretty bad shape again, in spite of huge doses. I've switched brands once but I think I'll have to switch again to crystalline."

"I'm sorry to hear that," said the superintendent politely and it seemed perfunctorily to Cyrus, but he was probably imagining things again. "I suppose you've considered . . ."

Cyrus watched the two men as they stood talking in the doorway. The tall meticulous figure of Willoughby looked almost insignificant beside the little cockatoo-tufted man with his piercing black eyes. Funny how unimportant size could be. Willoughby was quite a man to overshadow, but Everett's vitality almost equaled Miss Faine's. Hell, it had to for him to run a hospital the way he'd been running this one for the past ten years. Keeping the interns in line, keeping the chiefs happy and the politicians out of the trough. Everett was quite a guy per inch and per pound. It wouldn't be funny if in those ten years Miss Faine had run up against him more than once. Take a woman who wanted power and a man who just naturally assumed it and put them in opposing position like that, and you had dynamite. The fact that Faine had only been directress for a short time didn't make any difference either. As Kenny had often said, she'd been directress in everything but name for years.

"If her blood sugar isn't down again by afternoon, I'll be tempted to call in de Grasse," Willoughby was saying. "I don't know what he could suggest but I'd rather share the responsibility."

"He'll have something to suggest. He always does." There was dry humor in the superintendent's voice. "And speaking of responsibility, Les, how are you going to like taking over the Department of Medicine at the University?"

"I?" Willoughby raised his eyebrows with elaborate surprise. "I thought de Grasse ... I've been hearing some talk." But he couldn't suppress the eagerness in his voice.

Why, the guy wants it, Cyrus thought. And why the hell not? When you've worked like Willoughby you're due for a little glory, a lot more due than a chip-heavy, born-to-luxury guy like de Grasse. The trustees might not think so, though. Willoughby's reputation was with doctors, while de Grasse's was with people who were impressed by wealth and social position and prestige patients, and the trustees might be that kind of impressionable.

"Possibly de Grasse originated those rumors."

42

Everett's voice was still drier. "What I've been hearing is that you can't miss, short of murdering an important patient, of course."

Willoughby shrugged. "The trustees dispose and they're an erratic crew, but we'll all know by the first of next week. Not that it really makes much difference. What I'd like to know now is your opinion of Miss Faine's condition."

Cyrus watched the two men curiously as they approached the bedside. Funny how chiefs could drop the medical question in hand for the rankest triviality and then pick it right up again where they left off. Well, they'd better pick it up quick this time and do something with it or else . . . He glanced at the sick woman.

Her burningly dry face confirmed his thoughts. She was too ill to speak but her sunken eyes, violent with the effort of trying to get out some idea, kept going restlessly from Willoughby's face to Everett's and back to Willoughby.

"How is our patient this morning?" Everett was saying awkwardly. "You must get better, you know, Miss Faine. The hospital needs you."

The muscles of her face grew tenser, her color deeper. She was trying to talk with all the intense will in her, but the words wouldn't come. There was an uncomfortable silence as they all waited, then

43

Willoughby's voice came soothingly, "Don't try to talk, my dear. We're all taking care of you. We'll have you well in no time."

Still she strained to talk, then suddenly lay limp on the pillow. And then, as if the gathered effort was now able to break through, a mumble of words came. "I'm not beaten," they sounded like, and then "Les, Les, you'll see . . ." Then she couldn't say any more. Cyrus hoped she was right, but he didn't at the moment believe it.

He was relieved to hear a noise at the door and see the monkeyish face of Miss Kenny peering anxiously in. He moved over to speak to her, glad to get out of the oppressive atmosphere.

"Your friend's not doing so good, Kenny," he muttered. "No damn reason, she just isn't. Willoughby's stymied, and when he doesn't know the answer . . ." He shrugged.

"I brought her mail," said the nurse in a rather dreary voice. "But it doesn't look as if she'd feel like reading it right away, does it?"

"Nope." Cyrus shrugged again. "Unless a look at your lovely face does what insulin has failed to. Ouch, I'll report that to headquarters. Unprofessional conduct on the part of a head nurse." For Kenny had pinched him where she could get the best purchase.

"How about it, Cutter? Something sinister in the

44

urge to pinch?" Dora Cutter and Miss Markham had joined them at the doorway. "Suppressed passion, wouldn't you say?"

"Or unsuppressed malice," Dora Cutter smiled her serene smile. "Pinch him for me too, Miss Kenny."

Miss Markham's round face wasn't amused. "Here is that crystalline insulin Dr. Willoughby ordered, Dr. Harvey," she said disapprovingly. "It just came up."

"Thanks." Cyrus had a sudden impulse of his own to pinch. God, how he hated correct nurses. He took the bottle from the head nurse and gave it to Evelyn Moore with instructions about the dosage.

It was one of those days which dragged into one of those nights. Cyrus felt, when he finally got to bed, that he had spent most of his time in the corridor shuttling between Men's Medical and the Nurses' Infirmary. And every time he reached the Infirmary there were more people outside Miss Faine's door, and every time Miss Faine was worse.

By noon she had lapsed into complete unconsciousness, and though the last report that had come in had shown a lower blood sugar as if the crystalline insulin might be going to help, the next one was up again and her physical condition showed no improvement.

Dr. de Grasse, coming over about four to consult on the case with Willoughby, for once could suggest nothing that hadn't been done. He tried. He looked down over his fat cheeks and spoke of infection and the various kinds of insulin. He smoothed his well-cut vest over his fat stomach and spoke theoretically about the various possible physiological changes that could bring about a condition like this. He suggested tests that could never have had any bearing on the case and that Miss Faine was now too sick in any case to undergo, and he made Cyrus want to stick a pin into him and let out a good portion of the hot air. But he didn't suggest anything that could lower the blood sugar or bring the directress out of coma. And the caffeine and coramine which he suggested as heart stimulants and which Willoughby had already ordered were admittedly last resorts. By noon the next day it was obvious that only a miracle could save Miss Faine, and the miracle didn't occur.

V

EVEN SO, Cyrus could scarcely believe it when the thing happened about nine that night. Evelyn Moore was filling a syringe with insulin for a final desperate dose that Willoughby and de Grasse standing by the bed had agreed upon. Dr. Everett was standing over by the window, his face expressionless. The hall was full of nurses. Cyrus knew why they were all there. Yet when Willoughby suddenly turned away from the bed and said, with roughness in his usually clear voice, "Well, de Grasse, I guess we've a lot still to learn about diabetes," his first emotion was indignant disbelief.

Miss Faine couldn't die. It was a definite insult to medicine, an impertinence on the part of nature. Miss Faine hadn't any business dying with science at

47

the helm. And science had been at the helm, and science knew its way very clearly indeed through the rough waters of diabetes. But she had died. He glanced at Willoughby straightening up from listening with his stethoscope, glanced to see if Willoughby shared his feelings, and his bewilderment at the death turned to bewilderment at its effect on Willoughby.

There was a stricken look on the chief's face, an odd sagging that was somehow out of proportion to the death of a directress of nurses, even this directress of nurses. Why, the old boy minds this like hell, Cyrus thought curiously. You'd think he'd be used to death by now. But he isn't. Maybe it's the blow to his pride. He isn't used to losing diabetics, isn't used to his diabetics even going into coma, but you wouldn't think he'd mind this much, not Willoughby.

He glanced curiously at Evelyn Moore, and found her face not so much stricken as unbelieving and frightened. She had the look of a sleepwalker who had been waked by some horrible circumstance. She was moving over toward Willoughby, the insulin bottle still in her hand, her steps as mechanical as a walking doll. Cyrus stood watching. What was she going to do?

When she got in front of Willoughby she gave a hard metallic little laugh. "Well," she said, "it's all over, isn't it? I ought to be glad for her, but I'm

48

not, because she wouldn't be glad. Funny she should have wanted to live, but she did. She loved living, loved fighting life. It never occurred to her that she could ever lose. And she didn't have to lose this time. You could have saved her if you'd really tried." She was looking straight at Willoughby. Cyrus realized it was the first time he had ever seen her look directly at anyone. Her eyes were dark, darker than her aunt's and now they were burning with almost as great an intensity. "Why didn't you save her so she could keep on fighting, fighting the world, for me?" she asked childishly.

"Miss Moore," said Dr. Everett putting his hand gently on her shoulder. "You're not yourself."

She looked at him then and moved out from under his hand. "No," she said, "how can I be—ever?" There was a hate in her eyes. You couldn't tell whether it was specific or general, but it was there. And then suddenly she put her hand to her cheek in the old familiar gesture and began to sob, long hard shaking sobs.

"Harvey," said Dr. Everett quietly, "take Miss Moore out and give her a sedative. Have one of the nurses put her to bed."

"Yes, sir," said Cyrus. As he got his arm around the slim shoulders of the sobbing girl, he could hear Everett saying to Willoughby with a sort of forced heartiness, "You mustn't let this worry you, Les.

49

You did everything you possibly could. We all know that. We're a hundred percent behind you." And de Grasse's booming bombastic voice, "Of course, of course. Naturally I came on the case a little late to contribute anything myself, but it's clear Willoughby had left no stone unturned. I shall tell the other men so." And that was a funny way for them to talk.

"There's only one way to explain it," Willoughby was answering in as tired a voice as Cyrus had ever heard. "The girl must have suddenly become insulin fast. I can't see why she should have any more than you can. Her diabetes had never been very severe and we watched her night and day from the moment she began to have symptoms. But that's what must have happened all the same. It does happen, you know." There was a brief defensive note in his voice. "You read any number of case reports." He breathed a tired sigh. "I could wish it had happened to almost any other patient. Miss Faine is a great loss to us all. I wish I could think of something else I could have done, but I can't."

And of course he can't, Cyrus thought resentfully as he led the girl toward a group of white starched figures part way down the hall. Nobody's going to blame him. Nobody could think of blaming him.

But apparently they could. The nurses were so busy whispering they didn't even see him approaching with the shaking girl. "Willoughby's supposed to be the best diabetic man in town," Kenny was saying, her brown face wrinkled up to look more like a monkey than ever. "He ought to have been able to prevent this if anyone could. I still can't see how it happened. Caroline Faine was the most co-operative patient I've ever known."

"It almost seems as if there must have been some sort of negligence," Miss Markham's shrill voice was contributing. "Miss Glade over on Medical did happen to say yesterday that he hadn't seemed quite himself since all this talk about the Chair of Medicine started. Ambition can be a terrible thing, I always say."

"Willoughby wouldn't let that interfere," Kenny defended without conviction.

"But something must have gone wrong."

"Yes, something must have gone wrong. Somebody slipped up somewhere."

Cyrus paused on the outskirts of the group, fighting down an impulse to beat their heads together. Miss Moore, still shaking with sobs, seemed oblivious to the conversation which, Cyrus thought, was nice for her.

"When you girls have finished with that reputation you're worrying," he said distinctly, "you might remember that people do still die in diabetic coma. If you ever looked at a text book you'd know it happens a lot more often than people realize. It's a tragedy. We all think so, but if I hear any one of you hinting that it was anything but unavoidable I'll personally slap her pretty cap off."

They had all turned toward him and he glared at them for a moment. He turned to Kenny. "Don't be a damn fool," he muttered. "There are enough of them already." Then he said aloud, "Will you put Miss Moore to bed here and give her a nembutal? She's pretty much cracked up." He let go of the shaking girl, then, seeing she was still clutching the insulin bottle, "Here, kid, you won't want this," he said, and dropped it into his pocket.

He turned to Dora Cutter who had been watching the performance with her clear inquisitive gaze. "Women," he said disgustedly, and strode back into the dead woman's room. But it wasn't just women. Everett and de Grasse thought the death was avoidable. You could see that. At least they thought Willoughby had been less than ordinarily skillful. And even he—well, God knew they had done everything they could think of, and people did still die of diabetic coma as he'd reminded the nurses, but not when they developed it in a hospital right under the noses of several hundred doctors.

He didn't remember the bottle of insulin in his pocket till he was on his way to his own ward to write orders for the night an hour or so later. Not till he was reaching in his pocket for a cigarette. Then his fingers touched the cold glass instead of paper. What the dickens? Oh, sure. He pulled the bottle out and looked at it.

Here was the stuff that should have saved her— and didn't. And why didn't it? There couldn't be anything wrong with the stuff. After all, it was the third brand they'd tried and, as Willoughby said, all insulins were pretty thoroughly tested. Tested? Lord, yes, he looked at the bottle curiously. All those stamps and seals and control numbers. It had to be good. Insulin Reg. U. S. Pat. Off. Control number, 94459. Sally's telephone number, all but the first. Whitbourne 4459. It couldn't have been night before last he was sitting in a movie holding Sally's hand. It couldn't have been he that was doing it. He stood there looking vacantly at the bottle for a moment. God, he was tired. If he could only stop thinking about diabetes.

The stuff had to be all right and yet . . . He'd never had a chance to test that first bottle, what with it's being thrown out. Well, damn if he wasn't going to test this one, crazy and all. It would just make him feel better somehow. Because something was queer. Those blood sugars. Down right after they switched brands the first time and then, why gosh, down a little after they changed to crystalline, but not for long. It was damn funny. It all added up to something. He was too tired to try any more to figure what, but it wouldn't hurt to leave this bottle at the lab tonight and have an animal test run off tomorrow. Nobody need know he was being such an old woman, and he'd feel better knowing at least that the insulin was okay.

He stood looking at the bottle with its tight rubber cap. Wonder what insulin tastes like. He turned it upside down and shook it a little. Not that tasting would tell anything. Nobody ever tasted insulin. Nobody ever even smelt it except maybe the lab men who sealed it up in these little rubber-stoppered bottles. Nobody could check up on it now but the lab. Or couldn't they? He could get some out with a syringe of course and . . .

You'd think insulin had more taste to it than that—tasted just about like plain water. Of course it wasn't a chemical, only an animal extract in some sort of preservative. He tasted it again. No taste at all. Maybe . . . He went to the icebox and got another bottle of insulin and drew some out of that onto the other hand. Nope, insulin just didn't have any taste—but wait. This time there was a queer after taste, a sort of rough numb feeling—like formaldehyde. It hadn't been there with the other stuff, or had it? Maybe he hadn't given it time to be there.

Well, he put the ward bottle carefully back in

the icebox. The test would tell the story. Tomorrow afternoon, and that was a hell of a long time to wait.

He stood looking at the bottle he'd taken from his pocket, and then almost as if it were a compulsion he squirted the syringe dry and filled it again from that bottle. Sixty units would be a good dose. He ought to go over to the lab and have a blood sugar first. He was too damn tired, but nothing to stop him from taking a good shot and seeing what sort of reaction he got. He could always take sugar if he began to feel funny and by the time it would happen he'd be lying comfortably in bed. Kind of interesting being a guinea pig yourself for once, hell of a lot better than waiting till tomorrow.

"Oh, Dr. Harvey," there was a breathless voice at the door. "We've been phoning all over the hospital for you. That man with the heart block is getting awfully blue again." It was Miss Jones, the night nurse, a pretty kid, but kind of easy to scare.

"I'll be right there," he said. "Go get some morphine ready," and started to put the syringe down. Do this later. No, the hell with it. He shot the stuff into his arm. He'd go see that man and then get some sugar and get to bed.

He went with tired steps into the ward. Miss Jones hadn't been easily scared this time. He was so busy for the next couple of hours that all thought of his own personal experiment was swept from his mind. Before he had the heart block really under control a bad pneumonia was brought in and he had to phone all over the hospital for an oxygen tent and start the man on sulfadiazine, a new drug he and Willoughby were experimenting with, and see how he tolerated it.

It was a lot later when he straightened up for the last time and heaved a sigh. He had both those babies where he wanted them for the night—out of danger at least. Why the hell should you care? Bums both of them, no good to anybody, even themselves. But cripes, when you played tennis you didn't ask the ball whether it wanted to fall inside the little white lines or not. These guys could take their lives and like it. Plenty often the balls landed outside, plenty often, Miss Faine for one. Gosh, there was something he'd been meaning to do about the Faine business. Oh, sure, that insulin. But he had taken it, hadn't he? He glanced at his watch, three o'clock? That couldn't be right. He couldn't have been at these two cases five hours. Because if it was five hours he ought to be in shock already.

Sixty units of insulin and he hadn't felt a darn thing. And the first bottle had been thrown away, and . . . His mind was full of blood sugar figures, up and then down; then up, up, up, then down a little; then up again; and up and up and pfhtt.

He took the bottle out of his pocket again and looked at it, the bottle with Sally's telephone number on it. Well, this one was going to go safely into the lab icebox and be tested first thing in the morning. Funny it should have tasted so much like plain water. Well, so had the other, or had it? Not quite. Oh, he was nuts. Probably he had some queer insensitivity to insulin. He and Miss Faine, eh? But drug houses wouldn't go around putting water in insulin bottles. Nobody would. What the hell for? What—the hell—for? He stopped so suddenly he all but fell over. Lots of reasons, for a person like Faine. Oh, lots of reasons, only things like this just didn't happen.

VI

THE pathologist stepped back from what was left of Miss Caroline Faine, once directress of nurses in the City Hospital, and motioned to the orderlies to sew up.

"Well," he said calmly, "you didn't really expect to find anything, did you? Never do in a diabetic. Always makes me wonder while I'm posting one what in hell actually made the heart muscle stop contracting. This one's typical. Nothing, not a damn thing, but there she is." He waved a casual rubber-gloved hand toward the slate slab. "Of course miscroscopically the island cells in the pancreas will show degenerative changes, but then that's no news."

Willoughby sighed. "No, I really didn't expect to

find anything. But there might have been a bad gall bladder or some other hidden infection, maybe even a brain abscess, to account for that sudden resistance to insulin. It's been a very disturbing case, Jefferson. I'd blame myself if I could think of anything else we could have done, but"—he sighed again and shrugged—"I haven't been able to."

Cyrus didn't say anything. Not because he hadn't anything to say but because he had too much, and because an autopsy room full of people bending over slate slabs, delving into the causes of dead bodies being dead bodies didn't seem quite the place. The atmosphere was too damn scientific and what he had to say, while plenty scientific in its way, wasn't going to sound so. Not at first anyway, and especially not till he got that report from Foster on the animal test. Resistance to insulin, fhooy. Of course there hadn't been any infection or other cause. You didn't have to be resistant to insulin if you weren't getting any. He glanced at his watch. Foster ought to know by now. If he could just hold Willoughby till he called the lab and then get him alone for a moment.

Screwy, in a way, this furtive feeling he had about the business. Why not come right out with it? Only if, as he was pretty sure, but still found hard to accept, Miss Faine actually had been murdered, the police or somebody ought to know before everybody else found out. Because if there was a murder there had to be a murderer and . . . Cyrus had never read a detective story in his life. Just existing had always been plenty exciting so far. His mind wove clumsily through the probable processes of murder and discovery. Almost anybody else, he realized, was better prepared to cope with a situation like this. Only nobody else seemed to have any idea that there might be a situation to cope with.

Funny Willoughby hadn't, with that diagnostic mind of his, except that murder is something that just doesn't occur to you. Gosh, Cyrus thought, it hadn't occurred to him until the facts were staring him practically in the face. Or hadn't it? Watching Willoughby reach for his coat, wondering how to get him to wait and listen, Cyrus suddenly realized that his subconscious mind must have suspected something right after the disappearance of that first bottle of insulin. Not that he put as much stock in the subconscious as Dora Cutter, but no one could honestly believe, as he had pretended to, that three bottles of insulin could be defective all in a row. And a guy isn't very apt, however research minded he is, to give himself a big shot of insulin if he really thinks it's going to give him a hell of a reaction.

Cyrus stood there a little bewildered by the hidden mental processes that could apparently go on without your brain knowing about it at all.

Probably those subconscious processes were what made a diagnostician a good diagnostician. Yet Willoughby was famous for his diagnosis and his subconscious hadn't told him anything was wrong. Maybe nothing was, either, but he'd stake his last quarter, and here it was right in his white ducks, that something was going to show up.

Probably Willoughby had just happened to be reading a couple of reports on insulin fastness, and couldn't think of anything else. You couldn't exactly blame a guy for not diagnosing an apparently simple case of aggravated diabetes as actually a case of premeditated murder. You couldn't, as a matter of fact, blame Willoughby for anything this morning, the way he was looking. Funny, he should look so awful. Maybe not so funny. He'd seemed actually to like the female, and then there was the blow to his professional pride.

Willoughby was on his way to the door. However he was going to tell him this thing, he'd better get to work and tell it before the guy was gone.

"Dr. Willoughby," he called, "I want to ask your opinion about something, but I have to call the lab first. Could you wait a second?"

"Can't it wait, Harvey? I'm late for my office hours now."

"It's pretty important, sir." Cyrus caught up with him at the door. He could feel the other men in the room watching him curiously and stepped outside and pushed the door closed as casually as he could. "It's about Miss Faine. There are a couple of kind of strange circumstances I'd like you to . . ."

Willoughby smiled wearily. "Nothing about Miss Faine can be very imperative now," he said. "Tell me tomorrow."

"It can't wait till tomorrow." As Cyrus saw his chief's eyebrows go up in rebuke he added in a rush, "I don't think Miss Faine became insulin fast, sir. I don't think she was getting any. Someone had been deliberately tampering with her insulin, I've discovered."

That got Willoughby's attention which was something, even though it was pretty amused attention. "Come now, Harvey, you've been reading the *Daily Mirror*. We don't have arsenic rings every day, you know."

"We don't have people die in diabetic coma often either, not when they've been under the constant care of the best specialists in the city. You've got to listen to me, Dr. Willoughby. I've got proof."

"Go ahead, Harvey." Willoughby stood still, his overcoat in his hand.

"It's pretty complicated, sir." Cyrus took a deep breath. "You remember when Miss Faine first came to the Infirmary we talked about her insulin possibly being defective. You changed the brand, and

62

I thought I'd have the old bottle analyzed just for fun. Well, when Miss Moore went to get it it had vanished. That's the first thing. The next thing is that both times you changed the insulin her blood sugar went down, and then pretty soon went right up again. I didn't think much about that at the time, but last night when Evelyn Moore went to pieces she happened to have the last insulin bottle in her hand. I took it away from her and later, in the ward, I began to wonder if it could be defective too, so I took a shot myself, just to see. I was going to have an animal test run but I didn't want to wait. I took sixty units, Dr. Willoughby, and I didn't get any reaction at all."

"Sixty units is a pretty stiff dose." The chief's voice was skeptical. "You were risking quite a reaction, if you really took that much."

"I figured I'd be in bed by the time the reaction set in, but I was kept up with that heart block and then the pneumonia. If I had collapsed it would have been right on the ward, but I didn't. I didn't feel a thing. Whatever was in that bottle, Dr. Willoughby, it wasn't insulin. I think somebody has been substituting bottles of plain water for some time. It wouldn't have been hard to do."

"Where is the bottle now?" The chief was still skeptical but at least he wasn't impatient any longer.

"At the lab. I had Foster run off an animal test

first thing this morning. That's what I wanted you to wait for, till I could call him and get his report."

"Call him now." The chief lowered his voice as they moved back into the autopsy room. "I'd talk as discreetly as possible on the phone, Harvey. This is a pretty serious thing to go spreading around before you're sure. And it's going to be fairly hard to prove even if you are sure."

"Not if the report . . ."

"Well," the chief smiled drily but his voice got still lower, "that would help, but even so I can imagine people saying you were cooking this up to save my reputation. I don't want to be unpleasant, but you've cooked things up before, you know. It could even be said that you and I were cooking this up together. If it's true, we'll have to investigate it, of course, but we want to be pretty sure we've something to investigate."

He stood by the phone while Cyrus lifted the receiver and said, "Chemistry, please." And waiting for the connection, as you always had to, Cyrus studied his chief. If he had looked worn before he looked more worn now. His eyes, always a little prominent behind their rimless glasses, were more than usually bulging, and his stiff collar, the hall-mark of Willoughby, some interns said, looked as if it was holding his head from dropping over. Tough to take, Cyrus realized, the idea of one of

64

your patients being murdered. Bound to be a stink about it. Saving your reputation as a diabetic specialist, maybe, but at what a price . . .

"Hello, hello, Dr. Foster there? Hello, Harvey speaking. What did you find on that sample I left in the icebox?" His words were noncommittal, but suddenly his voice rose. "Listen, you couldn't have. I took sixty units of that stuff last night and didn't feel a thing. You what? What? Well, look, can you wait there till I get over? I want to see for myself."

He turned back to Willoughby, scowling an almost dazed scowl. "Let's get outside," he murmured as he saw the curious glances of the other men in the room. When they reached the comparative privacy of the hall, he said, "Foster says the stuff gave a perfectly normal insulin reaction at two testings, but I don't believe it."

Willoughby smiled. "I do. People, generally speaking, don't commit murder, Harvey. I'll admit resistance to insulin is unusual, but it's a good deal more usual that both you and Miss Faine were resistant, if you took as much as you thought you did, than"—the smile became wider—"that there was foul play. Let's just forget about it, shall we?"

Cyrus' face grew dark red. "I admire you a lot, Dr. Willoughby, but if you think I'm making all this up to save your reputation you flatter yourself," he said rudely. "I know you're busy, but I'm busy too. I didn't get to bed till three this morning and I've a lot of work still to do over on the ward. And as for those scandal sheets you're talking about, I never have time for the damn things. This isn't my idea of recreation."

Willoughby's smile stayed on. "Let's put it this way, Harvey. I think you've a theory that is quite interesting, and that for all its unpleasant connotations I'd almost like to believe. But I don't think it stands critical analysis. I'm sure when you consider the matter you'll see for yourself that it doesn't. I don't dare support it, because the very fact that I'd like to believe it would lay me open to the charge of trying to save my own face, particularly at this time." He emphasized the last three words.

At this time, with the Chair of Medicine sitting there empty and de Grasse waiting to pounce. So that was it. Pretty intelligent of Willoughby, preferring to live down a charge of incompetence rather than let anybody say he was trying to find an out. Pretty intelligent, but still . . .

"You can't just ignore a thing like this, not if it's murder."

"If it *is* murder." Willoughby was growing impatient again. "You haven't one shred of evidence, Harvey, except your overdeveloped imagination. The insulin proved perfectly normal. The autopsy

66

showed nothing out of the way. Your theory doesn't hold water, and I'd forget it if I were you."

"I can see your side of it, sir," Cyrus spoke earnestly, "but I know there's something wrong there and I'm going to find it." He grinned. "If you'd feel like a fool trying to prove something was wrong, why I'd feel like a worse fool not trying. You'll never stop doubting my ability to measure a dose of medicine or to diagnose an insulin reaction now, if I don't. I think I'll run up to the lab and see Foster."

VII

FOSTER, a baldish, dried-up-apple sort of man, looked up with a grin when Cyrus burst into the lab a minute or so later. "What you trying to prove, Harvey," he said, "something about negligence among the drug houses? Guess you picked the wrong bottle to prove it by. Look." He walked over to a cage where some rabbits lay somnolent on their sides and indicated a chart tacked to the top. "See that drop of blood sugar? That one came after the first shot, and here, look at this other drop after the second. I gave a third shot about an hour ago and . . ." He gave a short hard chuckle as one of the rabbits began to twitch. "Looks like this little devil is going into hypoglycemic shock, in case you want some more proof."

68

Cyrus stood and looked at the animal. It was showing all the reactions he had looked for in himself last night without finding. It didn't make sense but there it was. He looked and then shrugged. "I'm convinced," he said. "Give the poor devil a shot of glucose and bring him out of it. Wait though, sure you got the bottle from the lower right-hand corner of the icebox?"

"Lower right?" the chemist faced an imaginary door and reached with his hand. "Yeah, way in the back, and there isn't another bottle of insulin around anyway. Why would there be? They're all tested before they're distributed." His voice was patronizing.

"I know. Can I have another look at the bottle?"

"Looks like any other one I've ever seen." The chemist picked it up from the marble-topped table. "What's all the mystery about it?"

"Like any other?" Cyrus ignored his question, turning the bottle over, frowning thoughtfully, and suddenly he stopped. "Not to me it doesn't," he said staring at it, muttering numbers to himself, "not by a damn sight. Look, Foster, I don't blame you for thinking I'm crazy. Of course the test was normal, because . . ." He broke off, his eyes narrowing. "Look, go on over to lunch and forget my troubles. I'll buy you some cigarettes if I ever have an extra two bits. And," he grinned, "I'll tell you all about this if I ever work it out myself. Mind if I take this along as a souvenir of my bad judgment?"

Foster shook his head. "They get crazier every year," he murmured into space. "Must be a saturation point, but doesn't seem to be." Then to Cyrus, "You coming to lunch?"

"I'll be along later. There's something I have to do." Cyrus' voice was vague. He'd go back to Willoughby and show him the bottle. He'd show him the number that last night had been Sally's telephone number all but the first; 94459. Whitbourne 4459. Hello, is Miss Sally Pepper in? He could see the little red figures dancing before his eyes as they had first struck them last night. Whitbourne 4459. But he didn't know any telephone or street or any other sort of number that read 96870. You didn't go around imagining things like that. If it had been just one number off, or two, well, perhaps. But all of them, all but the first? No, you couldn't be that far off. Somebody had changed that bottle during the night. Somebody—somebody that must have known he had it. Somebody—well, obviously the murderer.

As his long steps carried him down the corridor in the opposite direction from lunch, his mind went back to the scene of the night before when he'd taken the bottle away from the weeping niece. Who had been there? Practically everybody when you got right down to it. He could see the crowded hall, the knot of gossiping nurses, the doctors going in and out of the dead woman's room. Almost anybody could have seen him take that bottle away, well not quite anybody but certainly one of a dozen or two people, and he wouldn't even know who most of them were. Let's see now. Willoughby? But that was crazy, and anyway Willoughby liked the woman. Everett was all over the place about her too, and so was the squirrely niece. Funny, when he'd first thought about it last night, he'd felt that lots of people would want to murder Miss Faine, but when you got right down to it what you meant was that lots of people ought to want to, but apparently nobody did. Even Kenny, who was usually so hard boiled, seemed to have a soft spot for the old gal.

Who else now? de Grasse? Miss Markham? And then a lot of other nurses and a couple of orderlies and—and Dora Cutter. He could see Dora Cutter's serene face as he had said, "Women," in his utter disgust. There had been a satisfied look to her face almost. Oh, he was going off his nut. Just because she had said she thought Miss Faine was a menace didn't mean she'd actually commit murder to save her precious students from the directress's sadistic discipline. Lord, no. Cutter was swell. But maybe just because of that she'd be the kind of person who'd want to play God and get rid of someone she thought was hurting a lot of people. Cutter? He saw her serene face and dismissed the matter. Much more likely one of the student nurses who had been so beaten down she'd gone off her trolley, or even one of the graduates who had been nursing a grudge for awhile. One thing was certain: It had to be someone who knew the hospital, someone who could have got at Miss Faine's insulin without anybody suspecting.

Well, the first thing was to tackle Willoughby all over again. He'd have left the hospital by now, but you could call him at his office. Cyrus' hand closed over the little bottle. At least he had something to show now, at least he had definite proof. Or did he? Call Willoughby and he'd probably say, "I can't go to Dr. Everett with a cock-and-bull story like this. I've only your word about those numbers, Harvey. You've been known to cook things up before." He could hear Willoughby's light voice, see his dry smile.

Nope, chances were Willoughby still wouldn't go to Everett, but nothing to stop your doing it yourself. Everett had horse sense. Everett wouldn't think he was making all this up for some screwy purpose. Everett wouldn't be afraid to face facts either. Look at the way he'd fought those politicians last spring over their using the free hospital beds. Fought them and beat them down. Everett wouldn't shut his

72

mind to an unpleasant possibility just because it was unpleasant.

But twenty minutes later he was standing in front of the desk of the dynamic little superintendent, and the superintendent was smiling as he sipped a glass of milk from the tray in front of him, and whether Bliss Everett had shut his mind to an unpleasant fact or not, the fact certainly hadn't got home.

"You know, Harvey," he was saying in that deceptively gentle voice of his, "I've been superintendent of this hospital now for ten years. I've had interns come to me because they thought patients were trying to starve themselves to death and because they thought the dietitian was trying to starve the interns to death. I've had them tell me that nurses were holding grudges against them and that nurses were in love with them. I even had one, once, who thought a patient was putting the evil eye on him. That was a Lancaster County boy. And I've often had them ready to be given over to the police because they felt they had inadvertently murdered a patient themselves. But I never really expected, you know, to have one of you come to me with the tale that somebody else had murdered one of his patients, and if I had, I really wouldn't have picked you, Harvey, unless," his smile vanished, "this is another of your mistakenly quixotic attempts to see that justice is done. Fortunately none of your other attempts have resulted in harm to anyone, though I'm glad to have this opportunity to let you know they have not gone unnoticed. But murder is a pretty serious charge, Harvey, even when it's not against any one specific person. I'd let it alone if I were you. If it's the gossip about Dr. Willoughby that is bothering you just remember that gossip never hurt anyone unless he is vulnerable. It'll soon die down."

Cyrus had always snorted at the expression "about to burst." Physiologically unsound he had called it more than once, but now he reversed his opinion. People did burst, of course they did, because he was going to. But bursting wouldn't put this thing across. It would just be futile and kind of messy. He took a deep breath and let it out slowly.

"Dr. Everett," he said, "I know I've run pretty close to the wind a couple of times, and I'm sorry as hell now that I ever did. I can see what people mean all right when they talk about living so that no breath of suspicion can ever touch you."

Dr. Everett had been listening, his eyes fixed on the intern's face. Now they shifted, and his face became a mask, and that was funny, part of Cyrus' mind registered, but the rest was too preoccupied with his own problem to pay attention. "I can see that I haven't," he went on, "but you couldn't honestly think, sir, that I'd make all that up about taking the shot of insulin, about the different numbers on the bottle. And I couldn't have made it up about the blood sugars going down every time we changed the brand and then going right up again because that's right there on Miss Faine's chart."

"Have a sandwich, Harvey." Dr. Everett's face was still a mask. It was as if he hadn't heard a word that had been said. "The diet kitchen always sends me enough food for a gorilla, and you must be hungry if you came here instead of going to lunch."

"No, thanks, sir." It wasn't often that Cyrus wasn't hungry, but now he was too painfully bewildered to feel anything as simple as hunger. "Don't you at least think we ought to put the case before the police and let them decide if there's anything to it?"

"No, Harvey, I most certainly don't." Dr. Everett bit into a cheese on rye. "If there actually should be a murder here it would be a very bad thing for the hospital, but we would have to undergo the processes of the law in the interests of justice. It would, however, be a great deal worse for the hospital if it got around that someone, a scatter-brained intern if you'll pardon my quoting the hypothetical press, had thought there was a murder and then was unable to prove it. Miss Faine's sudden lack of response

75

to insulin is an unusual circumstance, I'll admit, and it is very natural for you to be puzzled and disturbed about it. But there is a great deal about diabetes we still do not know. Dr. Willoughby has explained it to me and even shown me case reports of this happening without warning or explanation. Dr. de Grasse is also satisfied that this is one of those mysterious cases. And you yourself have admitted that the insulin you suspected tested entirely normally.

"As for the rest you have told me, well, I'll tell you what I think. I think you've had a pretty heavy schedule and been under quite a strain with this extra case to look out for. I think your natural and very splendid loyalty to Dr. Willoughby has warped your usually sound medical judgment. I don't think for a minute you're making all this up, but I do think that when people are tired and under a strain they sometimes are a little vague about circumstances. I think you may have a peculiar insensitivity to insulin yourself, or have taken less than you thought. I remember how often I read hypodermics wrong when I was an intern. And as for the matter of the number, well, when as pretty a girl as Miss Pepper is involved, it seems perfectly natural to me for a tired young man to see her phone number on everything he looks at."

"Well, look, sir." Cyrus' voice was ragged. "You

76

do admit the death was unusual. You might as well because the whole hospital is gossiping about it."

"Yes." Everett sounded exhausted. "It was unusual."

"And you have just said that whatever fool things I've done my medical judgment is usually pretty fair. Well, then, you couldn't think I could get so many facts wrong all at once."

Everett got up abruptly. His face was taut and there was a stiffness in his whole body. "There is nothing else for me to think except that you are deliberately trying to falsify facts to save the face of your chief and possibly your own rather overdeveloped vanity. You say Foster okayed the insulin. You say Willoughby sees nothing in all you've told me. Well, Harvey, I don't see anything in it either and I'm rather tired myself today. Miss Faine was a very old and valued associate of mine, so if you'll excuse me. . . Of course if you should find anything more conclusive I'll be glad to talk to you again, but"—his smile was far from friendly—"I scarcely think you will. I suggest that you get someone to relieve you and have a good twenty-four hour sleep. Women, I have discovered, aren't the only ones who get the vapors."

"Thinking a murderer's at large doesn't make for very good sleeping," said Cyrus, and knew he sounded childish even before Everett said, "Perhaps after a little sleep you won't feel quite so sure, and if you do and have picked the culprit come let me know."

Cyrus turned to go. "Oh, by the way," said Everett in a new voice, "how is little Miss Moore bearing up? I'm afraid this is going to be quite a blow to her."

Cyrus stared. The superintendent's face was soft and almost warm all at once, as if he had completely forgotten the unpleasantness of the last fifteen minutes. But he was in no mood to wonder about irrelevant nuances. "I haven't seen her since Miss Kenny took her off to bed in hysterics," he said rudely. "As you yourself have pointed out I've had other things on my mind."

VIII

It was four o'clock in the afternoon and Sally Pepper was knocking lightly at the door of one of the private rooms in Nurses' Infirmary. She had been knocking for almost a minute, but though there was a little card on the door that said *Evelyn Moore,* there had been no answer. Sally was torn between opening the door to see if the girl was asleep, and slipping away. Probably Evelyn wouldn't want to see anyone, but nobody as withdrawn as that ought to be allowed to bear her tragedy all alone. All day she had been trying to find a moment to slip up to the Infirmary and at least say "Hello." Sally balked at the officiousness implicit in her action, but she balked still more at the thought of

79

that still, strained face lying alone, thinking bitter thoughts. She knocked a little louder.

"If you want to see her you'll have to walk right in," said a calm voice. "But I'm not at all sure she'll talk to you. She's been lying there all day in almost a trance-like state, refusing food and practically refusing to be washed or cared for."

Sally looked up into the inquiring brown eyes of Dora Cutter. "Do you think I'd better leave her alone?" she said.

"No, I wish you'd go in and stir her up. Do her good whether she likes it or not—that is, if you can stir her up. Just open the door and walk in." The resident moved away with her athletic stride, but for all the woman's candor Sally was left with an impression of being used. She almost turned and went back to the clinic, but then the face of Evelyn Poole came before her again, and after all a psychiatrist had a right to use people to a good end. She opened the door and went in.

She found the girl lying motionless in the bed, her eyes closed, her hair loose around her shoulders. And what pretty hair, she thought, remembering almost with resentment the way it had always been strained back and pulled into a knot. What a pretty face, really, in a queer elfin sort of way, now that the strain of facing the world was momentarily absent. What a shame people of this sort couldn't lead the protected lives they were probably born to lead. And that was a funny thought, because the rumor had always been that Evelyn led too protected a life, too protected by her aunt. Oh, but the wrong sort of protection, not the sort that made her feel protected, but the sort that made her feel shut off.

"Hello, Evelyn," she said softly. There was no answer so she stood silent for a minute and then went on. "I just came to tell you how much we've all been missing you down at the clinic and to bring you a message from a couple of the children. Jimmy Murphy says, 'Where's Miss Poole? She'd want to know about my dog having puppies. Tell her I'll give her one if she wants.' And Jessie Johnson, you know the black one with the cast on her foot, cried this morning because you weren't there while the cast was being changed. 'I want Miss Poole," she said. 'She'd keep it from hurting me.' So I hope you'll soon feel well enough to come back. You seem to be pretty important down there."

She had been talking along nervously in the face of absolute lack of reaction from the girl in the bed. Now she stood silent, wondering what to do next. Perhaps, she thought with faint impatience, if she pinched her . . . But then Evelyn opened her eyes.

"I have the strangest feeling," she whispered, as if she were talking to herself, "a sort of lightness, a sort of free floating feeling. That's why I haven't wanted to open my eyes and look at anybody or talk to anybody for fear it would go away. It must be the sedative they gave me last night when—when I went all to pieces. I ought to be ashamed about that, but it seems so far, far away and long, long ago. Do you think it is the sedative that makes me feel like this, or," her voice was childishly naive, "do you think perhaps I might be going to die too? Aunt Caroline always said I'd never be able to live without her and I was sure it was true." There was momentary terror in her eyes. "Do you think that's why I feel this way? Do you think two people can be so close that one actually can't live without the other?"

"Heavens, no," Sally's voice was brisk to shake off the almost spooky mood that had been coming over her. "That light floating feeling is partly the sedative and partly relaxation. You've been living at high pitch day and night for almost four days, you know, concentrating on being as good a nurse as you knew how. The reaction would be bound to be tremendous.

"Look," she went on gently, "why don't you just lie there and keep on floating and let me brush your hair and maybe rub your forehead a little." She went to the bureau and got the girl's brush and began to stroke her hair. "You've such pretty hair,"

82

she rambled on inconsequentially, "you really oughtn't to hide it the way you do in that tight knot. A funny thin little face like yours needs something around it. You ought to wear it a little looser and see what the children say."

After about fifteen minutes she went to the bureau and got a glass. "Look," she said proudly, "see how different you look when your hair isn't screwed back."

The girl opened her eyes and took the glass. She looked for a long moment. Then suddenly she threw the glass from her. "Oh, I couldn't," she said, and turned her face away from Sally into the pillow and put her hands up to sweep the hair back from her face again. "It would be too dangerous wearing it that way. They—they might like it, and I might want them to like it and then—and then . . ."

"They?" said Sally softly. "Who do you mean by they, and why shouldn't you want people to see you looking pretty? Tell me, Evelyn." But the girl had shut her eyes and was lying motionless with her hand up to her face and she didn't seem to hear anything more that Sally said.

She left the room after a few more attempts and went down to the clinic with a depressed feeling. It was grim seeing anyone so alone that the loss of an aunt like Miss Faine could affect her this much. It seemed as if there must be something more behind it, some reason for this terrific dependence and sense of loss.

Suddenly she wanted to talk it over with Cyrus Harvey. He usually had pretty good ideas about things, Hard Boiled did, and what a name for a man who held your hand all through a movie and then didn't even follow it up by trying to kiss you good night. Heavens, it had been a long time since that Monday night, only three days, but it seemed a lot longer. Cy had been awfully busy over this death, of course, but he might have found a moment some time in three days to say hello at least.

She turned the corner into the children's wing and saw a tall, white-trousered figure perched on the edge of Miss Kenny's desk, and her heart flopped over. Cy? She was crazy, there were a hundred interns in the hospital. This could be any of them, probably Roberts, the pink-faced children's intern. But nobody else perched that way. And most of the others were too afraid of Kenny's caustic wit to treat her so familiarly. Three days since she'd seen that crazy, crooked-mouthed cluck and it ought to have been a relief, but her heart was pumping unnecessarily. She approached the desk. It was probably someone else anyway.

"Hello, Hard Boiled," she said casually. "Who's gossiping this time?"

84

He looked around at her and grinned, but it wasn't a very infectious grin, and the sockets of his eyes looked bruised. "Hello, Vassar. I've been looking for you. I've got troubles but nobody will listen to them."

"What makes you think I will?" Sally hoped that pounding business inside of her wasn't audible. After all, the guy was nicknamed Hard Boiled.

Sitting on the desk his eyes were on a level with hers. He looked straight into them, and that was always disconcerting, because you kept expecting his eyes to be brown and here they were that funny dark blue. "Because I know you so well," he said casually. "Besides, isn't that what you've been trained for?"

Sally looked away. "If you'll come out to my office, Dr. Harvey, I'll see what we can do about your case."

"He can spill it right here, if he wants," said Kenny. "I've got work to do anyway," and started to rise.

"No, you stay and listen." Cyrus pushed her down. "You might be kind of interested too."

Sally put on as alert an expression as possible to hide her disappointment as Kenny settled back and Cyrus began to talk. But when some fifteen minutes later he finished, "And the number was different, I tell you, absolutely different, but I can't get either

Willoughby or Everett to even listen much less take it seriously," the alertness was entirely spontaneous. Her eyes were wide and frightened.

"I know how they feel," she said slowly, "because it simply couldn't be true, not right here in our own hospital. The only difference is, I know you're not trying to put something over and they don't. Besides," she looked away, "I don't believe however tired you were you could be wrong about facts like insulin dosages and," her voice grew very casual, "telephone numbers. So whether it could be true or not it just must be. Don't you think so, Kenny?"

Kenny gave a bitter snort. "I've been around this hospital too long to think there's anything that couldn't happen. There's plenty of people who are a lot happier today with Caroline Faine gone. Only thing is," her words came slowly, "anybody who didn't have the guts to stand up to her wouldn't have had the guts to pull a thing like this. If it is murder, children, it's pretty close to foolproof, and you're never going to prove it. The only evidence is in that monstrous brain of yours, Harvey, and what a fancy piece of mechanism that is. No wonder"—she grinned a twisted sort of grin—"no wonder the chiefs are suspicious of it."

Cyrus shrugged angrily. "All right, if they're just suspicious of my sanity, all right even if they should happen to be right and I'm going around having

hallucinations, but what sticks in my gizzard"—
he frowned—"well, I understand how Willoughby
feels, he doesn't want it to look as if he's trying to
find an out. But it seems kind of funny that Everett
should be so hell bent on not seeing any sense to
what I told him. I can't help wondering . . . It's a
lousy thing to say, but maybe he knows more about
this than he's admitting, and this is a fine easy way
of shutting me up." He frowned again. "If I thought
that, hell I can't think it, but if I did . . ."

"It's a fancier piece of mechanism even than I
thought," Kenny all but snarled. "It not only smells
out a damn improbable murder but then starts fit-
ting it onto the only decent intelligent guy who has
been around this hospital in the last twenty years.
Good Lord, Harvey"—she paused and shrugged
angrily—"you're just looney, that's all."

Cyrus stared. "That lead pipe you have for
arteries, Kenny, turns to macaroni in the damnedest
places. Faine, and now Everett, what a pair to choose
to act human about. Next thing you'll be going soft
about me."

"I don't feel it coming on, and I'm not going soft
about Everett, but I've seen him in action a good
deal in the past ten years. He's just a sound guy,
that's all."

"Well, ignoring Everett and his remarkable obtuseness, will you tell me what you'd like to do

about this? After all, Miss Faine was your friend, not mine."

"Proving it was murder and not inefficiency isn't going to bring her back." Kenny's mouth was still bitter. "Do? I don't want to do anything. I'm not much for abstract justice, Harvey. I've lived too long and seen too much to believe in it. She's dead, and that's that. I'll miss her like hell, but I'm no avenging angel. I'm not interested in stirring up a stink. I'm interested in keeping my job and"—she paused and looked away—"my health."

"Your health." Sally gave a gasp. "Cy, I hadn't thought that far, but she's right. If there has been a murder, maybe you've been talking right to the murderer sometime today. Maybe you've even been telling him that you, you alone in the whole hospital, suspect there has been a murder."

"Talking right to the murderer! Look, Sal, you make me look like a piker. You aren't thinking that Willoughby or Everett could actually . . ."

Sally lifted her hands unhappily. "No, not really, only if you're going to believe one impossible thing you have to be ready to go on from there. Kenny's right, Cy. It's dangerous, terribly dangerous. Drop it, please drop it unless you're ready to go ahead and call in the police."

"Lot's of good that would do. They'd just repeat what Everett and Willoughby have said. Two emi-

88

nent specialists have agreed the deceased was insulin fast. The insulin tested okay. Everything is perfectly usual and regular. The police aren't famous for their imagination."

"And you are." This was Kenny, and her voice was quiet now. "I don't say you have to be wrong about this, Harvey. Me, I still kind of think Willoughby just slipped up somewhere. But even if you're right and I'm wrong you can't get anywhere."

"She's right, Cy." Sally put her hand on his arm. "Let it alone, please let it alone. You're just sticking out your neck. You're just asking," her voice faltered, "for another murder."

"I'm used to sticking out my neck." Cyrus grinned sourly. "But even I can see when I'm up against a stone wall. The hell with the hospital. The hell, begging your pardon, Kenny, with the late lamented Caroline Faine. If the chiefs want to leave a murderer at large to save a few headaches and a little scandal it's all right by me." He got to his feet with a wry grin.

"Come on, kid, you're going to eat with me because if you say no I might burst out crying. And you're going to eat with me now and in the interns' dining room because I'm too broke to take you out. Sure, it's only five-thirty, but that's when interns dine. See you, Kenny."

"Look," Sally was gathering her things up from

her desk in the clinic waiting room. She hadn't protested about dinner. It hadn't seemed any time to protest, but now the vision of a hundred interns watching her enter a room with this hard-boiled cluck was too much. "Look," she said, "let me take you out for once. You need a little isolation, I'd say."

Cyrus grinned down at her absently. "My ethics let me eat off your upper-bracket family, kid, and what eating, but not off you. Screwy distinction, but it's there. And if you're worried about the boys, they won't even notice you tonight. It's me they're laying for. You ought to have had a load of the whispering and snickering and head-shaking that's been going on among interns and nurses ever since this thing leaked out, God knows how, this morning." He grinned again. "You're insulation, kid. Maybe if I have a lady in tow . . ."

Sally started silently across the court with him. "Look," she said again halfway across. "You really are going to let this thing drop, aren't you?"

Cyrus raised one eyebrow mockingly. "You're not talking about Miss Faine's death, my girl? Didn't you hear? She was insulin fast. Willoughby is going to write a report."

Sally looked up at him, but she didn't smile. "I'd like to believe it," she half whispered. "Gosh, how

I'd like to, but I know you better than that, Hard Boiled Harvey, son of old Humanitarian Harvey. You aren't even started, and heaven help," her voice almost disappeared, "us both."

IX

But she hadn't known she would need help quite this way or quite so soon, Sally thought unhappily as she sat fifteen minutes later picking at the City Hospital stew. It ought to have been funny. It would have been funny seeing a tough guy like Cyrus Harvey so thoroughly on the spot, if she hadn't been convinced by Cyrus that what these interns were having fun over was really tragedy and pretty sinister tragedy. If she hadn't known so definitely, and frighteningly moreover, that however willing Cyrus might have been to let the matter drop a quarter of an hour ago, he never would be now.

It had started the moment they walked into the dining room, with piercing whistles that died into

92

subdued derisive chuckles. Sally wished wretchedly that they had been able just to drop into empty seats at the women's table which was near the door. But she saw Dora Cutter look up with a grin, half companionable, half mocking, and knew enough of hospital convention to realize Cyrus would have died first. Cyrus sat her down with empty chairs all around them and Sally was grateful for the lateness that made those empty chairs possible, but they didn't stay empty long.

Jim Knight, who had been on Children's a month or so ago, picked up his canned peaches and coffee and came plumping down beside her. He grinned at Cyrus, then lowered his head confidentially toward Sally. "Look, Social Service, I'd be kind of careful about going around with this guy too much. Fast ones in the way of exposing a ward to measles to keep a kid in the hospital may get by, but when it comes to seeing a murder under every post-mortem sheet just to save the face of a lousy chief, why gosh, at that rate he might start committing them to prove his point."

"Yeah"—another one paused on the way out—"let the chiefs cover up their own mistakes is what I say. If Willie can't cope with a simple case of diabetes, hell, the world ought to know about it."

"And is it ever finding out," Tom Truley on Women's Medical joined in. "Nurse over on the ward says de Grasse told her he was doing everything in his power to stifle the gossip, but that unhappily there was always a certain amount of talk in cases like this."

Cyrus did rise at that. "Stifle it? I'll bet he is, with a broadcasting outfit from the nearest possible point of vantage to that empty Chair of Medicine. Stifle it! De Grasse gives me a swift pain in a vital spot and so do you—all of you. Not that I would expect any of you to know the difference between . . ." He broke off as he found Sally's knee suddenly and comfortingly close to his own. He managed to go on eating while the show went on.

"Call in the police yet, Cy, or think you can handle this better alone?"

"Been taking Social Service to view the body? Wish you'd taken me. Must have been quite a body."

"Let us know when you want to begin fingerprinting."

And, as a climax, Bob Morgan, who had been in with Cyrus on a hospital strike a month or so ago, but was always against any ideas except his own, came up with a paper orchid pinned to a paper figure of a not-too-young corseted female.

"A clue, Nero. Police depose that one of Nero Wolfe's orchids was found clutched in the hand of the corpse. Better send Archie to suppress the evidence, but," he leered at Sally, "when did he have his face lifted?"

It was as grim a half hour as Sally had ever spent. When finally they were practically alone, except for a few scattered serious souls who didn't think even suspected murder was cause for laughter, Cyrus turned to Sally and grinned sourly.

"Well," he shook a cigarette loose and held it up to her mouth.

"Well?" she replied soberly, with a rising inflection.

"Well, I'm sorry, kid, but a guy can only take so much."

"I know," she sighed. "Where are you going to start?"

"Damn if I know yet. That's the trouble. It's such a swell job of covering up. Even the police couldn't find any evidence, even if you could get them interested enough to look. Why, hell, if it weren't for that different control number I'd think I was all wet myself. But I can't rationalize that control number, so . . ."

"So what?"

"You mean so why? So why would anybody have done it? That's the only place there is to work from now."

"Well, revenge, jealousy, avarice, to quote my learned English professor."

"All right. Revenge? One of the students or ex-students she rode just a little too hard. Jealousy? Let's see, Miss Wiley fell into her shoes but I can't see Miss Wiley having the guts to commit murder, not without more incentive than being directress. It could be," he snorted at the thought, "a jealous lover of some sort out of the old gal's past. It could, but that's even harder to swallow than Wiley. Avarice? Well, unless she had a pile salted away—and when would she have had a chance to salt it? No, that's no good. Besides, who would inherit?" He was suddenly silent.

"Evelyn Moore," said Sally unwillingly.

"Yeah, and Evelyn certainly had . . . Oh, the hell with that, she was nuts about her aunt." He turned restlessly and stretched his long legs out beside the table. "Well, if it was murder, and I can't see it any other way, either somebody was at white heat because of something that just happened, or," he paused, "somebody had been harboring a grudge for a hell of a long time and just took this chance. Whoa now." He tapped his fingers restlessly on the table. "Didn't Evelyn say? Why, sure she did. She asked Willoughby, when the Faine first came to the Infirmary, if an emotional upset could have brought on the crisis, said her aunt had been very angry about something lately, something personal." His face drew

96

together. "Think you could get anything out of Evelyn, kid?"

Sally shook her head. "I could try, but she closes up like a turtle when you ask her anything. I could try, though, and I will, first thing tomorrow."

"Meanwhile," Cyrus looked restlessly around the room. The waiter was taking the things off the other tables as if they weren't there. There were a couple of doctors still at the women's table. "Hey, Cutter," he called, "come have a cigarette and help us delay George here. We need your brains."

"Thanks." Dora Cutter dropped into a chair across the table with her light mocking smile. "In connection with your—murder?"

"I suppose you think it's funny too."

"No, I'm apt to smile when I'm upset. My psychoanalyst said it was a fear of ridicule manifestation, and analysis should have cured it, but it hasn't. No, Cy, I think it's horribly serious because so horribly probable. I've had a frightful furtive feeling ever since I first heard the rumor at lunch time, because I've so often wished that someone would. You'll never know, either of you," her voice grew bitter, "what that woman could do to a shy, immature eager-to-please little student."

"That's what I want you for. You think a student could have done it?"

97

"I think several of them could have wanted to. I don't quite see any of them with the decision or brains to carry it through." The sentence ended on a rising note as if her thoughts were going on unspoken.

"You wouldn't tell, would you, Cutter, if you did suspect one special one?"

"I wouldn't want to." The woman was hesitant. "I don't think I'd actually shelter any one. Provocation and all, and there must have been plenty, murder is a pretty dangerous thing for society to shelter. No, I think I'd tell if I definitely suspected someone, but it would have to be definite."

"You kind of think I ought to let the whole thing drop, don't you? So does Kenny, so does everybody but"—he carelessly pulled a strand of Sally's hair—"but this little fool here."

Sally shook her head free and carefully lighted another cigarette. Dora Cutter shrugged slightly. "I'd probably let it drop, because I wouldn't have the courage to dig deeper. I'd be too afraid of what I might find. If there's been a murder, there's been a lot going on before to make it come to that. I think some things are maybe better left alone, but"—she smiled at him with sudden brilliance—"you don't need to tell me you aren't made that way. Thank God for a few intelligent extroverts."

"You haven't been going around all day, being

snickered at and sneered at," said Cyrus uneasily. "Men have died for less."

"And you just possibly might die for this."

Sally caught her breath. "That's what I've been telling him, but it isn't going to make any difference. He's going ahead, partly for his own reputation and partly for Dr. Willoughby's, but he's going."

"What about justice, not to mention curiosity?" Cyrus defended himself.

Sally shrugged. "Those come in, but about third and fourth."

Dora Cutter was soberly stamping out her cigarette in one of the thick saucers. Now she got up. "I'll gather together the things I've heard around the Infirmary. I've kind of a hankering for justice myself, and I've a lot of faith in those hunches of yours, Cyrus Harvey." She looked straight into his eyes and her own held sudden funny little lights. "A lot," she repeated.

"Which takes us right along to the old gal's past." Cyrus turned to Sally as soon as the resident had left. And doesn't he know she's in love with him, Sally thought with a sudden pang. She's not so old, only three or four years older than he is, and what a woman. Doesn't he know and what would he do if he did? But Cyrus was saying, "How the hell do you find out about the past of a man-hating power-crazy directress of nurses, huh, kid? Women trained here,

Kenny says. Maybe Kenny was here when she was. Maybe she . . ."

"Kenny isn't going to contribute a thing to this inquiry. She meant it when she said that."

"And she'll stick to it. Of course Kenny could just as well—" he halted—"just as well as anybody else," he finished lamely.

"Of course she *could,* only . . ."

"Listen, kid," Cyrus' voice was suddenly hard, "this is no parlor game we're playing and we've got to get over our squeamishness. If we're going to get anywhere we've got to suspect everybody, everybody. I know damn well, for instance, though Cutter didn't say a word, that she was thinking of Evelyn Poole. She's enough of a psychiatrist not to take all that intense devotion act too seriously. The kid's going to be better off without her aunt, a lot better off, and we don't know what may have been going on. Well, Cutter suspects Evelyn, and if you want to know, I've been kind of suspecting Cutter till just now. We've got to do it that way and that's why I'm going to need you. I can't figure this out without help, and you're about the only person I know with neither incentive nor opportunity, besides," he grinned, "being pretty fair company."

"Okay, sir," Sally swallowed hard. "So how are we going to dig into the gal's sinister past short of Evelyn, who probably will do a disappearing act when I start asking questions?"

"I don't know." The words came separately and unwillingly. "Wish I could even imagine the woman with a past."

"I can"—Sally shivered—"of some sorts." Then her face lighted suddenly. "Wait now, one of the nurses was griping about T.S.O. awhile ago, and she said they kept practically a life history on file of every nurse who had ever trained here so . . ."

"So Faine ought to be on file somewhere, too?"

"Maybe right there in T.S.O., in all those filing cabinets."

"In that case"—Cyrus got to his feet and pulled her up after him—"we'll let George sweep us out. I've got to crawl over to the ward for awhile, but if you'd be interested in going to a movie or seeing a sick friend or something for a couple of hours, I'd be delighted to meet you outside the Administration Building, at say nine, when things have quieted down around there, and do a spot of file cracking."

X

THE grounds were dark except for a few dim lights suspended high overhead between the buildings as Sally drove her car in at the tall iron gate, past the little watchman's box and up to the concrete open space marked Staff Only. The Administration Building, as she walked toward it, loomed up a dark mass, except for a dim light in the front hall where she knew the switchboard operator was on duty. She was shivering with cold and not quite fright, but an uneasiness more primitive and harder to cope with. If Cyrus was right, and she never doubted he was, a pretty nasty crime had been concluded right in these grounds in the last twenty-four hours. What was more, since the whole hospital seemed to know that Cyrus suspected it, the murderer probably did too, and the murderer wouldn't like it particularly and . . .

She started determinedly up the steps and stopped cold as a dark form appeared suddenly at the top.

"Hello, kid."

"Oh—Cy," she gasped and clung to his arm in panic. "This isn't my idea of fun."

"It isn't going to be fun." He drew her into the light of the glass door, and his face was sober. "I've been standing here wondering why the hell I was letting you in for this. I guess I just wanted a shoulder to weep on, but now I've wept and I know where I'm going, and the first place I'm going is back to your car and put you in it and send you home."

"Oh, Cy," Sally almost wept. "You can't. I've gone through all the shivering and the shaking part, and now you can't cheat me of the chase."

"I don't give a damn for your feelings. It's your cute little neck I'm worried about."

"Listen, chum." Sally was belligerent suddenly. "I'm an investigator by profession, and I'm going to investigate. If you try to send me home I'll scream and tell the watchman you were making advances."

"He'd believe you too." Cyrus hesitated, then made a sudden decision. "I won't pretend I don't want you." He put one arm around her and pulled her close and nuzzled his chin in her hair. "There's something to scream about. Come on."

The night operator looked up incuriously from her copy of *True Detective Love Stories* as they crossed the front hall.

"Miss Pepper has to get some important information from the office," said Cyrus offhandedly. "Will you call me in there if I'm wanted?"

The operator nodded and Sally sighed her relief. They went down a dimly lit hall and Cyrus with his flash light found a door marked *Training School Office.* It was unlocked.

"Knew it would be. Dropped over after I left you and tried the door just to see." He opened it and switched on the lights. "Here's the office of the secretary of her highness the directress, and cripes, look at those files." There was a solid bank of them against one wall. "Must be something in all that locked steel."

"How about keys?"

"They must be around. You look in here and I'll root around in the queen's office. Pray nobody else is snooping, will you?" He disappeared. "Kind of plushy in here," she could hear his voice running on. "Oriental rugs and a carved desk, velvet curtains and a velvet cushion on the chair. Gosh, Cutter ought to see this. She'd write a case report. Maybe if Faine hadn't sat quite so easy she'd still be sitting. Any luck out there?"

"None so far," Sally's voice came from the bottom

of a deep drawer. "Lots of hairpins and lipstick and I wouldn't tell you what all else but no keys."

"No luck here either. I'm starting on the second row of drawers. Woman used a perfume called My Sin and that's pretty funny. Whoa now, behind a box of junk here . . ." He came to the door jingling something. "Enough keys to open the whole hospital and she probably did frequently." He handed them to Sally. "Where do we start?"

"The files are dated. Praise God, the woman was methodical, but," she paused, "what date?"

"Date? Let's see. Gal was thirty-nine. Say nineteen or twenty years ago, around 1921. Flaming Youth in the person of Caroline Faine." His voice was derisive.

"Here's one marked 1920-1924." Sally began trying keys. "Only one type seems to fit these files, but the dickens of a lot of them." She worked in silence. "Here's one that gives." She pulled the drawer open. "Why don't they tell you detecting is this easy? Can't be anything incriminating at this rate."

"Probably not." Cyrus shrugged as he found a manila envelope labeled, *Faine, Caroline* and pulled it out. "But there must be information of some sort. Look." He handed her half the cards. "You go over these. I'm starting with her health record. Not likely to tell much, but might as well be thorough."

He began to run over the chart with a practiced eye, grinning faintly as he came to certain notations.

"Fairly normal female, it seems, no diabetes then, no nothing as a matter of fact, all the first year. Second year," he started another card. "Here's a lot of attached correspondence. Looks as if the gal was out for six months. Incipient T.B. Went to her sister's and here's a note from her sister about it. Funny if she had a sister she didn't come around when Miss Faine was sick, or to claim the body or anything. Damn funny if you ask me."

"Maybe she's dead. That was nineteen years ago."

"Maybe, but if she isn't I'd sure like to see that sister." He began to scribble on a slip of paper. "Mrs. Thomas Hillsley, Tod's Corner, Pa. That's only about fifteen or twenty miles out. We're going to find out if the dame is alive right now." He started to turn the leaves of an out-of-town phone book lying on the secretary's desk, "and if she is . . ." He began running down a page. "Well, fancy that now, Mrs. Thomas Hillsley, Tod's Corner. She seems to have stayed put and alive. Kid, tomorrow after supper you and I are going to run out to Tod's Corner and find out from Mrs. Hillsley why there is such a lack of sisterly contact between her and Miss Faine."

"We?" Sally looked up from her part of the record. "Of course you wouldn't know that I have a date tomorrow night, with a banker."

"If money comes first with you it's time I found

106

out. I'll get Cutter to go. The thing's going to need female guile."

"I'll fix it up." Sally recanted with less than Whitbourne finesse. "He was only an assistant vice president anyway and . . ." She broke off and her eyes widened, for the telephone was ringing. They stood motionless, listening.

"Better answer it," whispered Sally after a moment.

Cyrus started toward the phone, then stopped. "Suppose it's for Miss Wiley. Maybe everyone wouldn't take our explanation of being here so placidly as that dumb switchboard wench. Maybe"— the phone was still ringing but he turned away from it toward the door—"maybe I'd better drop outside and find out who it's for. Lock the door, kid, and don't let anyone in whatever happens, till you hear my honeyed voice again." He grinned, but it was a forced sort of grin, then opened the door and went out. She turned the lock after him.

The telephone kept on ringing a few minutes and then stopped. Sally stood still holding the files, waiting for Cyrus to come back. When he didn't after a minute or two, she looked down at them and tried to start reading, but she couldn't stop listening and the silence out there in that dimly lit hall was almost harder to bear than a frank noise. Where was Cyrus? Why hadn't he come back to tell her? What was he doing? What was happening to him? She tried to look down at the big white cards in her hands, but her eyes wouldn't leave the door. Was it imagination that she thought she heard noises now, soft footsteps? Was it imagination that she thought she saw the door knob moving? She felt as if she were paralyzed. It wasn't imagination. Someone was trying to open the door. If they knocked or called to be let in, what was she going to do? She felt as if she were one long immobilized scream. Any moment the scream would come to life, and what then?

The door knob twisted one way, then the other way, then was still. She waited for the knock, but it didn't come. Then she heard, or thought she heard, little ghosts of footsteps moving along the hall again. Who had it been? What did they want? Where, for heaven's sake, where was Cyrus? Moisture was standing out on her forehead and the palms of her hands that were still clutching the cards. She dropped into a chair.

All time was the same till she heard footsteps again, but these were frank definite footsteps and she knew them. When a familiar voice said, "Okay, Sally," she found she was trembling so hard for a moment that she could hardly unfasten the lock.

He was grinning easily as he came in. "Call was for me. Something on the ward, something important, so I ran up and tended to it, knew it would only take a second. Everything all right here?" He hadn't really looked at her till now, and he whistled softly. "You don't look like it was. What happened, kid?"

"Oh, Cy," for the second time that night she was clinging to him. "Somebody tried to get in. I thought I heard footsteps. I wasn't sure, then someone turned the knob." He was silent. "You don't think I could have imagined it?"

"I know you didn't imagine it." His easy grin was gone. "I wasn't going to tell you, kid, figured you'd enough on your mind, but that call was a phony. Nobody wanted me on the ward. Nobody knew anything when I got there. Everything was quiet as little mice. Nurse couldn't figure out"—he smiled faintly now—"why I was so damn conscientious."

"What was the idea, do you think?" Sally looked puzzled.

He shrugged. "Get us away from here. Maybe just get us away long enough to destroy any of these records that might give us a lead. Maybe," his voice became deliberately matter of fact, "get us out of here and then lay for me on the way to the ward. I figured something like that might be on the cards, so when I scooted up there, I scooted a pretty roundabout way. One reason I took so long."

"Cy"—Sally's eyes became wide—"did you talk to whoever called, because it must have been . . ."

"I know, and that's the hell of it." He shook his

head angrily. "Whoever called, gave the message to the operator, and when I asked her about it she drew a blank. Didn't even know whether it was a man or a woman. Some one with a fuzzy voice, she said, but she thought one of the nurses must have a cold. I suppose we have *True Detective Love Stories* to thank for that missed bit of evidence."

"Evidence," Sally's voice was blistering. "I'd give a lot to know whether straight courage or lack of imagination explains you best. Don't you realize what you may have missed and may not miss next time?"

"Sure," he said, "that's why I went the long way around. Sure, I realize it. This is probably just the beginning." His face became suddenly solemn. "That's why I wish like hell you were out of it."

"But I'm not." Her voice was thin but steady, and she managed a sort of laugh. "How about those files?" Her hand was still shaking, but she managed to make her eyes focus on the cards again. "Let's get through with them and out of here. I was just finding out something important when that knob started twitching. Where was it? Here, listen to this, Cy. All your cracks about Miss Faine's love life, about flaming youth and all weren't as funny as you thought. Looks here as if she was quite a gal in her day. The incredulity in Sally's voice drove out the last trace of panic. "Guess who kept her out oftenest after hours. Just guess."

"Can't even think of that woman out with a man without getting gooseflesh. She'd suck his blood. What's this, interdepartmental memos?" Sally had silently handed him a number of little slips. "Between the then super of the hospital and the then directress, well, well." His eyes moved rapidly.

" 'Will you kindly speak to your resident on Neurology about his attentions to student Caroline Faine and inform him that she has lost her late privileges for the next month.' She would have a half-baked neurologist for a heavy date." He lifted the top slip and started another. " 'I have spoken to Dr. Everett. He was rather unco-operative but I have brought pressure to bear.' Everett, oh, for God's sake! Everett and Faine." He looked blankly into Sally's face.

"It wouldn't have to be Bliss Everett," said Sally automatically.

"But I'll bet it is."

"I don't believe it," Sally was suddenly vehement. "He may have had a date with her, but beyond that . . . To begin with, if there'd been anything more to it, whoever this Everett is, she'd have destroyed these records."

"Not Faine. She'd have got a kick out of having them right here and gloating about putting one over on the hospital. After all, nobody but she had the keys. Nope, kid, those memos don't sound to my nasty mind like a casual date. I can't quite figure

Everett as—but hell . . ." He broke off and his eyes went down to the cards in his own hand. He skipped over two or three, then stopped abruptly and looked up at her again.

"If you want something just as hard to swallow, something that makes me a little more anxious than I already was to get out to Tod's Corner, listen to who diagnosed that T.B. of Faine's and arranged for her to have sick leave to go to her sister's. A rising young internist, just starting practice he must have been, by the name of Lester Willoughby. Old home night here in the files, that's what it is, and I can't say I care for it."

XI

"WHAT do you think Evelyn will do now, Kenny?" Sally's voice was casual, but she wasn't feeling casual.

Sitting at your desk, getting ready for the morning clinic just as you'd done scores of times in the past year, it was hard to think in terms of murder. But this wasn't just any morning. This was Friday morning, thirty-six hours after the regrettable but perfectly understandable death, so everyone, or almost everyone agreed, of a highly respected superintendent of nurses. This was Friday morning following a Thursday night in which you and a certain dark sardonic guy, and guy was the only word, had done a spot of file cracking. This was the morning before the night you and that same dark sardonic guy were going to travel out to place called Tod's Corner.

There was a lot you had to find out, if you could, before you did that traveling. It was awfully different investigating the income and living conditions of a clinic family whose only possible interest to you was that it had a particularly sick or particularly sweet or particularly brattish young one, and investigating the past of a dead woman who had always given you the creeps, particularly when that past seemed to be tied up with someone you had always thought was just about tops.

What was the connection between Dr. Everett and Miss Faine, anyway? Even if it was no more than an occasional date, it was hard to go back twenty years and imagine these important dignified people as ever having been like Cyrus and herself. She could feel Cyrus' face in her hair as it had been that moment outside The Administration building last night, and it made her catch her breath. Hard? It was impossible. Miss Faine and Dr. Everett could never have been young, could never have been even that foolish, and, as for anything more . . . Still, there were those interdepartmental memos sitting in the file for her to take or to leave. Momentarily she left them.

There were plenty of other things to worry about. Dr. Willoughby? Well, that seemed perfectly clear. Dr. Willoughby had probably simply been Miss Faine's doctor for over twenty years. But what had she been in such a state about just before she was taken to the Infirmary? Why, if she had a sister, hadn't the sister come to see her when she was ill, or at least come to mourn when she died? Why was Evelyn Moore such a funny, frightened, withdrawn sort of person, and why in the world had she been so fanatically attached to that terrible aunt? Those were things to work on right now. If Kenny was the nearest thing to a friend the dead woman had had, she ought to be able to help with some of the answers, and she might be more co-operative than Evelyn Moore.

"What do you think Evelyn will do now, Kenny?" she repeated. "Come back to work or go away somewhere for awhile?"

Kenny shrugged. It was her most characteristic gesture. "Dropped in to see the kid last night. Wouldn't talk at first and then raved on about a free floating feeling like some lousy automobile ad, and did I think she was unnatural to be feeling that way or was it maybe the shock? Stuff like that. I told her if she'd put on her uniform and get down here to work she'd soon stop feeling so free. Told her we needed her, and that Faine would have been the last person to favor neglect of duty even in the name of grief, which, the Lord knows, was true enough. So"—she shrugged again—"maybe we'll be seeing her, maybe not."

"Aren't there any relatives Evelyn could go to? It must be pretty grim being all alone at a time like this." Sally's voice was still more casual. "Hard Boiled said Evelyn told him there was nobody else to notify, but it seems as if there must be someone. Didn't Miss Faine ever speak of any relatives in all the time you knew her?"

"Nope. But lots of people haven't any families, especially nurses. That's why they're willing to be nurses, nothing to do with lives of their own, if they had 'em. Nope, never heard Caroline Faine speak of a relative in the world but Evelyn."

"Well, I guess you'd know. You were in training with her, weren't you, Kenny?"

"I was out before she started, but I was around. Guess I knew Caroline Faine as well as anyone, but that wasn't too well. She lived to herself and for herself, did Caroline. Chief reason we were buddies at all, I guess, was I admired her guts of which she had plenty, and she got a lot of laughs out of me. I'll kind of miss her around here."

"Of course you will." The words were more polite than sincere, but Sally allowed a decent pause before she went on. "What was she like when she was young? Did she go out with men and things?"

"Caroline? With men?" Kenny gave an odd little laugh. "Why she . . ." Then she stopped abruptly. "Listen, Pepper, you're not this interested in Caroline Faine all by yourself. What you doing? Stooging around for that Harvey guy?"

"Why, no, I just couldn't help wondering . . ."
But Kenny ignored the weak protest.

"I wish like hell he'd leave this thing alone, Pepper. If there's nothing to it, he's only going to make a jackass of himself. And if there should"—her face crinkled up unhappily—"if there really should be, someone worked it all out pretty darn carefully. Someone might be smart enough to work something else out, and would probably just as soon, too. I'm scared, if you want to know, and I don't scare easy. Tell that guy to go pull in his chin. Faine wasn't anything to him. She was to me, sure, but I can't see a hell of a lot of difference between deliberate murder and hopelessly bad management of a case. Either way it ends in the post room." Kenny shrugged and her face was bitter.

"You and Dora Cutter," said Sally wonderingly. "I'd have thought both'of you would . . . Oh, well" —she imitated Kenny's shrug—"don't think I'm not wishing Cy'd leave it alone, too, but he isn't going to. He isn't made that way, so I might as well help him if I can, and you might as well help me."

"Far as Faine goes," Kenny was definite, "my mind's a blank and that's that."

"But don't you see, Kenny?" Sally started to reason with her but then stopped, for a blue and white skirted figure in a dark blue cape had just come through the door. "Why, hello, Evelyn," she said slowly. The girl's eyes behind her glasses were enormous with fatigue, but there was a faint color in her cheeks, and her face had almost the same relaxed look it had had lying on the pillow the afternoon before. Her hair was soft around her face, so soft you hardly noticed her glasses.

"Good morning," she spoke directly to Miss Kenny. "I came back—to help with the children."

"Good." Kenny was kind but impersonal. "We can use you. Dr. Roberts will be down in fifteen minutes to begin vaccinating. Go see that the stuff is laid out for him in the first cubicle." She gave Sally a monkeyish grin as Evelyn started toward the drug room. "Good fight talks, I must give."

"Yes," agreed Sally absently. All she could see at the moment was something like a double exposure; soft hair superimposed blurrily on slick strained hair in a tight knot, a soft mouth superimposed on a tight repressed one, color superimposed on dull pallor. It was a funny sort of change for grief to make. Was it a change that was going to make her information gathering, which so far had not been too successful, easier—or harder?

She had no chance to find out the rest of the morning. The clinic was an extra heavy one and all she saw of Evelyn was the top of her head bending over one child after another, or her back and shoulders hurrying to obey the intern's brusque orders. It was a relief in a way, putting off a disagreeable duty, but even more disagreeable was the awareness of passing time. So when the last child had gone and she saw the student throw her cape around her and start down the hall she reached for her own coat and caught up with her before they got outside the building.

"Going to lunch?"

"Yes." The girl brushed her hand across her forehead, but she was smiling faintly so that it gave none of the old impression of nervousness. "I'm tired, aren't you? It was a long morning."

"I kept wondering if you were going to be able to stand up under it." Sally's voice was sympathetic, and she felt sympathetic. She also felt a good deal like a heel as she went on, "Wouldn't it be a good idea, Evelyn, for you to take a few days off and get a little rest and change somewhere? I'm sure it could be arranged."

"Oh, no," the girl's voice was low. "There's nowhere I want to go. I'd much better keep on working."

"But aren't there some relatives you could stay with for awhile?"

Evelyn shook her head. "I've an aunt in the country somewhere," she said after a moment's hesitation, "but I never see her. There was . . ." She hesitated again and then went on as if under some compulsion.

"Aunt Caroline didn't want me to see her, ever. She did—she tried to do something dreadful to us, once, so . . ." She stopped. "I'm much better off working, Miss Pepper."

"But surely on the other side of the family. Perhaps your father's relatives." Sally had been busy filing away what she heard. Now she was amazed to see a sudden deep flush on the girl's cheek, but she stumbled on. "I do think a few days' rest would do you good, and I'm sure Dr. Everett could arrange with Miss Wiley to let you go."

"Dr. Everett." Evelyn put her hand quickly up to her face in the old gesture, but her dark eyes when she turned them on Sally were hard. "I wouldn't ask him for anything, ever."

"Why?" asked Sally, a certain departmental memo dancing before her eyes. *Will you kindly speak to your resident on Neurology about his attentions to student Caroline Faine.* "Why not?' she repeated softly.

Evelyn's hand had dropped from her face. Now she put it quickly up again. "It was silly of me to sound like that," she said nervously. "I just don't like to ask people for anything if I can help it, particularly men. Aunt Caroline didn't think much of men, and she told me, oh, I'm sure she was right too, not ever to be taken in by a pleasant smile. She told me," she went on earnestly, as if sincerity were getting the better of her nervousness, "there were only two things I could safely depend on, herself and work. Now"—she stopped uncertainly and blinked her eyes oddly behind her glasses—"I've only got work."

"What about yourself?" asked Sally. "You've got yourself."

"Why, yes," Evelyn sounded surprised. "I've got myself, but I've never thought of depending on myself before, because there was always Aunt Caroline. Why, yes," she repeated, "I have got myself."

"Evelyn," Sally spoke quickly, wondering how to ask it but knowing if she didn't now she might never have another chance. "Dr. Harvey says that while your aunt was sick you spoke of something that had upset her, something you thought might have helped to make her sick. Do you still think so?"

"No," said the girl apparently automatically. "Unless . . ." She broke off. "They say Dr. Harvey is trying to prove there's something queer about my aunt's death, to save the reputation of Dr. Willoughby. They've all been in to tell me that. That's just the kind of thing a man would do," she ended fiercely.

"That's the kind of thing a *man* would do if he thought it was the truth." Sally was vehement for a moment too. "You don't think it could be true?"

"How could it? I was with her every minute."

121

"Well," Sally started to explain, and then thought better of it. After all, Evelyn as well as anybody else, perhaps better . . . And it wasn't going to help to go into methods and theories now. "Did Dr. Everett have anything to do with upsetting Miss Faine," she said suddenly, "or Dr. Willoughby?"

"Dr. Everett?" the girl flushed scarlet and then turned suddenly pale. "Why, he, why . . . Why are you asking me all these questions?" she burst out. "I always thought you were my friend, and now . . . Oh, please leave me alone!"

"I want to be your friend, Evelyn. I'm only trying to find out. I only thought you'd want to know if . . ." Sally stopped, hopelessly confused in her motives, because why was she asking all these questions? Why did she want to find out all these things? Not to help Evelyn, not to help Miss Faine who was beyond help. Not, surely, in the name of abstract justice. That was more Dora Cutter's style. Then why? But the answer rose before her eyes only too quickly and too clearly and it was such an unsatisfactory, however overwhelming, answer that she went on hurriedly, "Oh, please don't let me upset you now when you've so much else to be unhappy about." She reached out and took the other girl's hand, and it was cold. She squeezed it hard. "Forgive me," she said.

"Hello, Miss Moore." It was a man's voice, but a gentle one. Evelyn turned her head and started to smile, and then turned it back again. "Wait a second." The voice was eager.

They were passing the interns' home. A white duck figure broke away from a group of white duck figures and hurried over to them. It was Henry Bowman, the resident on Psycho. Sally had seen him occasionally and heard more about him from Cyrus.

The resident's voice was full of concern. "I'm awfully glad to see you. I've been so sorry . . ."

"I know. I know you have." The girl looked up at him and her eyes filled with tears, and that was odd, thought Sally, who had been worried till now at the dryness of Evelyn Moore's grief.

"Look," Bowman went on awkwardly. "Please don't think I'm trying to rush you or drag you out in public or anything, but if you haven't any family around to be with, won't you go to the orchestra with me tonight? Music's a help. I know. Something like this happened to me a month ago. My father."

"Oh, I'm sorry, I didn't know that you . . ."

"Won't you go with me tonight?"

"I don't think"—the girl's hand went up to her cheek—"I don't think I could."

"Of course you could." Sally had been standing silent, watching. Now she broke in impulsively. "It would do you a world of good."

"But it wouldn't be right." Evelyn's hand was still at her cheek, but there was uncertainty in her words.

"It would be the rightest thing you could do."
Sally interrupted her and then turned to the shy near-sighted resident. "I'll work on her," she said. "It is what she needs. You call at the nurses' home for her at eight and she'll be ready."

"Why did you do that?" said the student with no apparent resentment, only a sort of wonder, as Bowman smiled and nodded and went on toward the interns' home. "I can't go, you know. He seems so nice, so different from most men, the kind of men Aunt Caroline used to talk about, but it wouldn't be wise. I wouldn't dare."

"Why not?" Sally's scorn was vehement. "Men aren't bugaboos. Men aren't any different from that nice gentle Bowman person—most of them. They just talk loud and deep and like to think they're big shots." She smiled suddenly for no reason. "You go with him tonight, and if anything terrible happens because of it, you come tell me, and we'll find some way of fixing it up. You do what I say now, see. I know what I'm talking about."

They were at the door of the nurses' dining room. She glanced at Evelyn and saw her cheeks were flushed again, and her eyes shining. The student nodded a little and slipped through the door, leaving Sally to realize that she not only had let slip a splendid chance to find out why Evelyn felt the way she did about men, but also had completely forgotten for a period of minutes that she was walking with and talking with a perfectly good suspect for murder.

"Match-making women," she muttered to herself, "make lousy detectives," and stalked on toward the social service dining room.

XII

DRIVING out along the old Limekiln Pike in her little green convertible some six hours later, Sally was darkly brooding. That she had plenty to brood about even the least imaginative and introspective person would have been willing to admit. To find yourself quite alone on your way to investigate a murder when it wasn't even, by any calculations, your murder, was bad enough, though Sally had had enough experience with life around a city hospital to swallow that. After all, there was a reason for calling interns interns. Their lives weren't supposed to be their own, and Cy couldn't exactly run away from a bad pneumonia, particularly a pneumonia he and Willoughby were doing a research job on, just to investigate a murder that nobody in authority was pre-

126

pared to admit existed. But there were plenty of other things to brood about.

She could still see the heavy straight line those hard-boiled eyebrows had been drawn down into when he met her outside the kid clinic and told her what had come up. They hadn't curved up any when she said calmly, "I'd better go anyway, don't you think?"

"Somebody ought to go," he had admitted. "This thing can't hang fire much longer unless we're going to drop it altogether. The stink about Willoughby gets stronger and stronger. Myself, I think somebody is encouraging it with a few well-aimed rotten eggs, but the trustees of the University meet on Monday, and if those eggs stick . . ." He shrugged angrily. "I'm a dope, but I like the guy. I want him to have that appointment and if he misses I'd a lot rather have it be for straight murder than for negligence that wasn't there."

"So I go," she had answered.

"Not alone, kid. Take Kenny."

"I'd love to take Kenny, Cy, but she wouldn't be any darn good even if she'd go. She's made up her mind this is something to be left alone and she's leaving it. She isn't remembering anything or saying anything. Maybe she doesn't know anything, but I've got it doped out as some crazy kind of loyalty. Nope, Cy, no Kenny."

"Well. Cutter then. She'd go. She might even have ideas."

"Yes." Sally's voice had turned unwilling. "She might go, but . . ."

"You mean we aren't absolutely sure. You mean you might be safer alone. I guess you might at that, though I'd sort of crossed Cutter off my list of suspects for maybe no good reason."

"She never was on mine," Sally had hastened to say, for she had balked at admitting even to herself that what had made her hesitate was all the unspoken things that would undoubtedly be passing between her and the tall serene woman doctor concerning a tough and not always too charming intern. "But I'll admit I'd be happier going alone, if I can't have you. After all, it's my job. I've got more information out of more reticent people than you could examine in a week of clinics, big boy. It's just my charm that makes you forget it."

"That must be it." He had looked down at her absently. "Matter of fact, you're probably safest of all without me for protection, what with that phony call I got last night and all. Nobody's going to suspect an orchid like you of going out to gather information alone, and it's perfectly clear somebody has his eye on me . . . So go to it, kid, but keep your peepers open."

128

"Yes, boss." She had smiled back to hide the panic she was feeling. "Any instructions?"

"Sure." She suspected his answering grin had had the same source as hers. "Try to find out what the female knows about Evelyn; whether she ever heard of Willoughby or Everett; what was the matter with Miss Faine that six months she was out of training. I looked through all the X-ray records for the year and couldn't find a trace of her name. Of course she might have had some taken outside, but they're expensive and it doesn't seem likely when she was a student here. And if none of those leads work, see if the sister looks like the kind of person who could turn herself into a hospital diet tray and transform the insulin inside a bottle into plain water. I've a hunch there's something peculiar between Faine and this sister of hers and we want to know what and why. That's all." He had waved his hand casually and let it drop equally casually on her arm. "Damn sulfadiazine, anyway. Why can't we let pneumonia patients die decently the way they used to?" His eyes had been warm and, for him, tender.

And, as if all that wasn't enough to brood about, Sally thought now, driving along, there was Evelyn's reaction to the mention of Bliss Everett, Evelyn's change, her blooming since the tragic loss of her aunt, and her general fear if not actual hatred of men, though Sally had an idea that the hatred of men was going to take care of itself.

But she wasn't going to have much longer to brood. She had just passed a sign saying Tod's Corner: one mile. Now what would be the best source of information at six-thirty of a March evening? The gas station? Well, probably.

The aging attendant scratched his head with one hand while he put in gas with the other, and when he began to talk Sally decided smugly that only a born investigator would have thought to leave the tank almost empty for just such an emergency.

"Mrs. Hillsley? You mean Maggie Faine who married Tom Hillsley awhile back?" Sally hardly had to nod for he went right on. "Guess you can't know her. Maggie lives right where they always lived at Barehill Farm down Twelvetrees Road, second road to the right when you get beyond the store. Not much of a place but she seems right fond of it, leastways she don't stir off it much, never did and less'n ever since Tom Hillsley died three years ago. Don't have much company either. She expecting you?" His little stone-gray eyes were bright with curiosity.

"No," Sally tried to project the proper note of solemnity above her rising excitement. "But a relative of hers died at the hospital where I work. We thought she ought to know."

"Now that's too bad." Curiosity leaped higher.

"One of the Faines? None of them around here any more, except Maggie that is, and she never was a real Faine, not in disposition anyway."

"Her sister, I think. Did you know her?"

"Well, I wouldn't say I knew her, if it's Caroline you're speaking about. She left here quite a few years ago. Hasn't been back." The man was suddenly cautious. "Maggie'll be right interested to see you, I bet." He finished wiping off the windshield. "That'll be one-sixty-five, Miss. Just turn to your right the second road beyond the store there. Can't miss it. Oh, Maggie'll most likely be at home. Like I said, she and Tom hadn't gone out much for the last ten years or so. Now she never does." He nodded agreeably, but Sally drove off with a feeling of hidden undercurrents and not too pleasant ones either. Barehill Farm sounded a good deal like a place you'd rather visit in company. But she had refused company and here she was and here was Barehill Farm. The sign was weatherbeaten and crooked and the lane was narrow and bumpy but maybe at the other end would be Information.

She turned in and headed the car slowly toward a small and not too well-kept farm house. A dog barked and her pulse speeded up. She was a good deal more afraid of strange dogs than of murderers, which was a pretty silly way to feel, she told herself, just because you've been bitten and never been murdered. That

131

thought didn't help her pulse rate any, but then she had to put on her brake to save the life of a fat and rather dirty duck who was waddling across the road, and you couldn't worry about a duck's life and your own all at the same time.

She was still smiling at the unshakableness of duckling dignity as she knocked on the peeling door of the frame house. It was opened after a moment by a small plump woman in an apron dirtier than the duck. Her curly dark hair was just sprinkled with gray but could never have been called distinguished. Her dark eyes had enough fire to mark her as Miss Faine's sister, but it was a warmer, more honest and less intelligent fire. She looked through the door without responding as Sally turned on the charm and said, "Are you Mrs. Hillsley?"

"Yes, I'm her, but you might as well know right now I buy everything from Sears and Roebuck." The woman prepared perfectly pleasantly to shut the door.

"I'm not selling anything. I came about your sister. Miss Caroline Faine is your sister, isn't she?"

"What about Caroline Faine?" The door opened again, but Hard Boiled had been right, Sally thought watching the woman's face, about the lack of sisterly affection.

"She"—Sally hesitated—"you probably don't

know then. She died the day before yesterday. I'm a social service worker at the hospital."

"No, I didn't know." The woman didn't show any sorrow or even pretend to. "I haven't seen Caroline for close to ten years. It's real nice of you to come all the way out here to let me know, but I guess if she's already dead there's nothing I can do." She prepared to shut the door again.

"No." Sally was frantically telling herself that anyone who had got information out of drunks and snow birds couldn't let a simple farmer's wife faze her. "But if you're Miss Faine's sister, you must be Evelyn Moore's aunt too."

"Evelyn." The woman drew in her breath and her expression changed, melted almost for just a moment. "How is Evelyn? How's she taking it?"

"Marvelously," Sally followed the lead quickly. "She went all to pieces at first, but then she pulled herself together like a soldier. Only she seems so terribly alone."

"Evelyn wouldn't want to see me." There was sudden bitterness in the woman's voice. "She hasn't been out here for ten years. She . . ." Her voice broke off and her face grew suddenly suspicious. "Say, Miss, you wouldn't have come way out here just to tell me Evelyn is taking Caroline's death right well. You must want something."

"Yes, I want something," admitted Sally speaking casually, but watching the woman closely. "We have reason to believe that Miss Faine's death may not have been accidental."

"Not accidental!" The woman's eyes widened but more with curiosity than with horror. "You mean somebody . . .

"We think somebody tampered with her medicine," Sally was going cautiously. "We thought you might know something about who would have had an incentive."

"No." The woman closed up suddenly. "No, I haven't seen Caroline for over ten years. I wouldn't know anything about it."

"Well, you see," Sally's words grew still more cautious, "Evelyn was taking care of her all the last days before she died. A good many people think perhaps she . . ." Sally had never known she could lie so glibly. "I don't, of course, but it's going to be hard to prove."

"Evelyn never did it." The woman rose to the bait. "She was crazy about that woman, not that she ever had any reason to be, but she was. She'd about have died for her. No, Evelyn never did anything to harm anybody." Her voice was shrill with vehemence. "There were plenty of other people who might have wished Caroline harm though, plenty."

134

"That's what I thought," said Sally, "and I thought perhaps you'd tell me . . ."

"I don't see as I've got any call to tell anything to a stranger like you, Miss. How do I know what it is you're after?"

"I've told you," Sally almost pleaded. "How would I know all this if I weren't what I said I was? If you won't tell me here, come with me to the hospital and we'll get Evelyn and she'll vouch for me. But you've got to tell me what you know. Evelyn"—she choked a little over the way she kept saying Evelyn when she meant Cyrus—"Evelyn may be in dreadful trouble if you don't. Come. I'll take you right in to Evelyn tonight."

"Evelyn won't want to see me," the woman repeated sullenly.

"But you want to save her, and if telling what you know will save her you must want to tell me. Don't you? Won't you?"

"No, I don't want to tell you," Mrs. Hillsley snapped suddenly, "but it looks as if maybe I was going to have to. Come on in." She held the door open unwillingly.

"Mrs. Hillsley," said Sally when they were seated in what was obviously the best parlor, "way back when you used to see Miss Faine, did she ever speak of a Dr. Willoughby?"

135

"Willoughby?" Mrs. Hillsley seemed to savor the word, as you would a once-tasted but forgotten delicacy. "Willoughby? Why, he was the one who brought her out here when . . ." She broke off and gave a short sharp and not in the least pleasant little laugh.

XIII

DR. WILLOUGHBY at this point was talking to his intern Cyrus Harvey on the telephone.

"Another one, eh, well, that's fine. That makes three on the ward now, doesn't it? Ought to be able to tell a good deal about the efficacy of that new drug when we see how these three shape up. What've you done? All the routine tests? Good. Good. Medication? Oh, you've already started the drug? Not doing so well, now? I don't like the sound of that. Well, Harvey, suppose I run out and look the man over. I'm particularly anxious to give this new stuff a good trial. I'll be out within a half hour."

You'd never have suspected that within the last eight hours one of these two abstract scientists had been trying to bring a murder to the attention of the

137

other and had been snickered down. And that was pretty funny, Cyrus was thinking as he put down the phone and went back to his patient. You'd think anyone as research minded as Willoughby would be research minded the whole way. Of course this sulfadiazine was Willoughby's research problem, while the peculiar behavior of apparently perfectly sound insulin was somebody's else, and even highly scientific gents were apt to be pretty jealous of or indifferent to other people's bright ideas. But that didn't sound like Willoughby. Maybe, as he had said, it was simply fear of looking as if he were trying to find an out. And then maybe it had something to do with his early, very early indeed, medical care of the late Caroline Faine.

Cyrus went back to his evening rounds while he waited. He listened to the heart of one patient and changed his digitalis orders. He went over the abdomen of a patient with cirrhosis, and found, with relief, that the fluid was decreasing. He looked over his charts and wrote night orders for his side of the ward, then wandered in to look at the newest pneumonia patient who wasn't doing so well. The man's temperature was still pretty high. He looked toxic and was beginning to show cyanosis around the lips, but Cyrus regarded him with none of the rising excitement, the tensing to battle that he usually felt, that he had been feeling specifically for the past

138

month whenever a pneumonia patient had appeared, to add one more statistic to his compilation of the effects of this newest germ killer.

Cyrus had always till now had a good deal of scorn for people who couldn't keep their minds on their work. He had never had any trouble that way himself. He was naturally a single-track person. But that was exactly the trouble tonight. He was on one track and the track wasn't running anywhere near Men's Medical where Cyrus was doing his restless pacing. It was following a small figure in a small green car out to a place called Tod's Corner, and when he managed to bring it back from there it started running, among other things, after a trio of insulin bottles. If Miss Faine wasn't getting insulin the last three days before she died, and Cyrus personally had stopped questioning that, why somebody must have made away with the insulin. And there were two ways of managing that. Either take the bottle on the spot and draw out the insulin with a syringe and substitute water also by syringe, which would be rather hard to manage with all the comings and goings of a crowded hospital, hard even for Evelyn Moore and practically impossible for anyone else. Or previously collect all the most usual kinds of insulin bottles, replace the insulin with plain water and simply switch the properly prescribed bottle for an identical one filled with water. Then the only remaining problem would be to dispose of the genuine bottle which would be no problem at all. A doctor could just drop it in his bag and even go ahead and use it up on other patients, if he were callous enough. And whoever did this had to be callous enough for anything. Of course the bottle taken from the lab icebox would be a little more difficult, but a doctor could still just drop it in his bag to dispose of when convenient. One insulin bottle, as Foster had so patronizingly remarked, looked much like another.

Yet it couldn't be one of the doctors. Certainly not Willoughby. Cyrus brought up a mental picture of his chief, the sharp light-blue eyes, the calm mouth with its dry smile, the keen mind. Willoughby had the mind to put something like this across all right, and he might have had the motive. But he couldn't have done it, he was too good a doctor.

Cyrus could remember his father saying a little pedantically but very earnestly once, "Remember, Cy, you can't be a sound doctor unless you're a sound person." They had been discussing one of Cyrus' more brilliant professors who had been caught falsifying some research findings. Cyrus had tried to defend him as a doctor, had poohpoohed his father's dogmatic statement, but he hadn't forgotten it. The old boy was probably right.

Cyrus' mind shied away to Everett. There was a hell of a lot of force in that little cookatoo-tufted guy, plenty of force to commit a murder—and there was that old tie-up whatever it was, and, please heaven, make Sally a smart enough investigator to find out what that tie-up was. But it was still pretty hard to see Everett and Faine, Everett nursing a jealous passion for that shrew of a woman for twenty years. And anyway, had he been around Miss Faine's room enough to make the necessary switches? Well, possibly. Would he have been able to get at the lab icebox without causing comment? Again, just possibly but not probably. Cyrus much preferred Everett to Willoughby as a possible murderer, but he didn't shape up as well.

Who else then? Cutter? Oh, she might do it if she really thought it was for the good of the whole, do it like a shot, but doing it for that reason would be psycho, and Cutter, for all her analysis, didn't seem really psycho. De Grasse, the big fat rich baboon? It would be swell to pin a murder on his red grinning face, but where was your motive? Discrediting Willoughby didn't seem quite enough.

Who else? Kenny? Miss Markham? Miss Wiley? Well, there didn't seem to be any motive. Evelyn? Evelyn looked awfully damn likely, if you could only prove that her devotion to Faine was a phony. Well, and it was a phony whether she knew it or not. Nobody could be genuinely attached to such a brute of a female, not unless there was some sort of outside pressure. Maybe Sally was finding that out. Maybe Sally was getting in trouble trying to find that out. Maybe . . . Hell of a note, this sticking around here waiting to stuff medicine down the throat of a guy who'd maybe be better off in the P.M. room anyway, when you wanted to be out digging in a place called Tod's Corner. Hell of a note. Sally'd be all right, of course. She'd have to be. Nobody knew she was going and no reason to think Mrs. Hillsley was a homicidal maniac, but still . . . Wonder how the hell Sally is? Wonder what the hell Sally's finding out?

XIV

MRS. HILLSLEY had fallen silent after that short and not in the least pleasant little laugh that followed her mention of the name Willoughby.

"Yes, we heard something about his sending her out here," prompted Sally softly. "Was that when she had the tuberculosis trouble?"

"Tuberculosis?" Mrs. Hillsley gave another laugh. "Sure enough, that was the tale they cooked up for the hospital, wasn't it? I'd forgotten that. Quite an imagination those two had. I'll grant you they had to think up something, but tuberculosis always struck me as such a quaint name to give to Caroline's trouble then." She stopped and looked at Sally suspiciously. "I'm not one for talking to strangers, Miss, and the Lord knows it's no trouble of mine to go messing around in. But if people are saying hard things about Evelyn, and my telling what I know can show them she's the last person to say hard things about in connection with that sister of mine, why tell I'm going to whether Evelyn will thank me for it or not."

"Oh, you must, Mrs. Hillsley." Sally was almost breathless in her intensity. "Somebody's got to tell the truth or we'll never get anywhere, and all sorts of horrible things may happen."

Mrs. Hillsley looked at her a moment with sullen eyes, then she said suddenly, "Caroline's trouble wasn't in her chest when that Dr. Willoughby brought her out here, my dear, but a little lower down, and it didn't take her but four months after she came to get rid of it, get well rid of it and leave it on my hands. I wouldn't have minded if she'd left it on my hands for good, for it was a cute little baby, and turned into as sweet a little girl as you'd ever see. What I resented and will resent to the last breath I draw, though Caroline is now dead and gone, was her leaving me Evelyn long enough for me to get fond of her and her of me, long enough for us to feel like mother and daughter, and then coming and taking her away again."

"Evelyn," Sally suppressed the exclamation. She mustn't seem surprised. She mustn't seem surprised at anything she heard, or anything she might be going to hear, or she might stop the flow of pent-up bitterness, the flow that was going to lead her, perhaps, to the cause of Miss Faine's death. Evelyn. She shouldn't even feel surprised, as a matter of fact. Why hadn't she thought of it before? Pretty dumb, pretty dumb and naive of both her and the hard-boiled guy. Why, of course Evelyn would be Caroline Faine's daughter. That would explain everything. Well, not everything, but a very great deal, and, she drew a breath of relief, it would pretty much rule out Evelyn as a suspect. Daughters, generally speaking, didn't go around murdering their mothers.

"And Dr. Willoughby?" she managed to say with only faint breathlessness.

Mrs. Hillsley made a wry face that would have been funny if there had been even a vestige of warmth in its humor. "Dearie, I wish I knew this minute about that elegant gentleman. I thought at the first the baby had to be his. A man, I said to myself, isn't likely to go to that much trouble for another man's bastard. But I saw a lot of him when Caroline's time came, saw a lot of the two of them together, for he delivered her himself, he did, right in there on the kitchen table with me pouring the nasty smelling anesthetic stuff out of a can onto a piece of cheesecloth for him, and Tom running around keeping the kettles boiling. And even at the worst Caroline made never a gesture toward him

145

that held either love or hate. And the way he acted toward her wasn't the way a man acts toward a woman, lawfully wedded or not, he's known well enough to give a baby to."

Sitting there listening to the uncompromising phrases, Sally felt almost as if she were smelling the ether, hearing the far from furtive wail of the baby that didn't yet know it had no business being born. Poor Evelyn, with a mother like that and a father . . . Mrs. Hillsley seemed awfully sure that Dr. Willoughby wasn't the father, and yet why else would he have gone to all that trouble, and it must have been a lot? Of course the Galahad complex, the Boy Scout instinct was awfully strong in some men, and Cy thought Willoughby was pretty swell stuff. She pigeon-holed the problem as Mrs. Hillsley went on.

"It isn't natural to go through a thing like that without showing any feeling, without ever in six months wanting to talk about it. For all Caroline ever showed, the baby might never have had a father, might just have been some kind of awful tumor she wanted to get rid of. But she was always an unnatural woman, Caroline. I knew it, and I wouldn't have taken her in to begin with if I hadn't thought what might happen to the baby if I didn't. Not having any of my own I wanted that baby. I was kind of glad when Caroline packed up when the little thing was only a little more than a month old, and walked out bragging that she was going back and marry the richest intern in the hospital. But her plans miscarried there for once, and I think it was partly rankling at having those plans miscarry that turned her so sour and nasty cruel later on. Caroline was never one who could stand not getting what she'd set her heart on. She couldn't even stand seeing anyone with anything she had a claim to whether she wanted it herself or not. I know that, all right, for she left Evelyn with us for ten years, and just as we were forgetting the little girl had ever been anything but our own daughter, Caroline came back one Christmas and took her away with her."

Sally had been as much fascinated in the last minutes by the apparently endless flow of cliches as by the story they were managing to tell, but now, as the woman's bitter voice grew deeper with a harder and uglier bitterness, she forgot everything but that this was the story of Evelyn Moore, forgot even for a moment that this might also be the story behind a murder.

"It was a Christmas Eve when it happened. She arrived as if she were just coming to spend a regular Christmas with us, as she always had. And then she took that child and went into this room with her and they talked for two hours, and when they came out the child wouldn't speak to me or to Tom, just looked at us coldly and blankly, not even crying and went with her mother, calling her Aunt Caroline in a sort of sad subdued voice, the poor little thing. I haven't seen her from that day to this. What could I do? The child was rightfully Caroline's. She had a right to board her anywhere she wanted.

"But it's my opinion that she deliberately poisoned the mind of that child against Tom and me, telling her we had driven her poor mother out in shame, telling her we had tried to separate mother and daughter. Oh, it wouldn't have been hard for her to do. And she could have kept the child tied to her like a slave for the rest of her life—and she'd have liked that too—by working on her shame at being a bastard and her sympathy for her poor mother's tragic betrayal by one of the wolves of this wicked world."

Mrs. Hillsley was all but panting as she finished the long pent-up tale. She sat there breathing hard, her eyes blazing. In a moment she said more calmly, "I haven't mentioned any of this to a soul since Tom died three years ago. I wouldn't now, except that I want you to see there's lots of people could have wanted to murder Caroline before her own daughter. And I want you to see that though Evelyn had plenty of reason, she'd never have even realized it, thinking as she did that her mother was sacrificing her whole life just for her."

"Things will be happier for Evelyn from now on," said Sally as gently as she could through her sup-

148

pressed excitement. "I had wondered why she seemed so different since Miss Faine's death, freer, happier, but frightened and ashamed of being that way. Mrs. Hillsley, I think you ought to come in and see her. She wouldn't believe these things from anybody but you, and she ought to know some of them at least. She's so terribly alone. I think she'd want you, if she knew you wanted her."

"If she knew," the woman still sounded bitter.

"But you could make her know, particularly when we get to the bottom of this—this murder."

"Murder," Mrs. Hillsley repeated the word almost meditatively. "Murder. Well, Miss, I don't know whether I'll come see Evelyn or not. It depends . . ." She broke off. "But you tell her I'm here if she needs me. Tell her I'll stand back of her."

"You can't give me any clue as to who her father might have been." Sally persisted. "I can't help feeling that's the most important lead of all. Didn't Miss Faine ever speak of any man, a Dr. Everett, for instance?" She got the name out almost by force.

"Everett?" Mrs. Hillsley considered and then shook her head. "She spoke of somebody once with a name like grass, or something. He was the rich one she was going to marry and then never did, but Everett . . ." She shook her head again.

"Did any friends ever come to see her in those six months while she was with you?"

Mrs. Hillsley started to shake her head once more. "Oh, there was one came a couple of times. A little dried-up thing with a face like a monkey. Caroline used to say she was the only person in the hospital with sense. I never knew her name though."

Sally knew. And so that was why Kenny wouldn't talk, she thought with a surge of affection. People said there wasn't any loyalty between women, but Kenny wasn't going to dabble even in murder if there was a chance of its hurting the reputation of her not-too-blameless friend. It was a strange relationship, but not so strange as some of the other relationships she had learned about this evening. She got up as casually as she could for the excitement in her, and held out her hand with a warm smile.

"I can't tell you what a help you've been, Mrs. Hillsley. I think you've very probably put us on the right track, and I'll certainly tell Evelyn I've seen you and what you've told me." But as she shook the woman's hand she was thinking that, except for opportunity, a better murder suspect never existed than this blousy little woman before her.

XV

DR. WILLOUGHBY was in the ward now with Cyrus, looking at the pneumonia patient who wasn't doing so well. There was a slight frown on his face. "I think what we'd better do, Harvey, is increase the dose further. He seems to have tolerated the last pretty well as far as his blood count and kidneys go." He turned to the nurse. "Will you get that bottle of mine from the drug room, please?"

A minute later he was shaking a square brown bottle and holding it up to the light and his frown was deeper. "You should have told me we were this low, Harvey. There won't be enough here to last through the night if we increase the dose, hardly enough for all of them even if we didn't. How did you happen not to notice it?"

Cyrus stirred on his feet uncomfortably. He knew darn well why he had happened not to notice it, and so did Willoughby, though he pretended to ignore it. Maybe he hadn't been the perfect intern in the past twenty-four hours or so, but try to be a perfect intern and single-handed detective all at the same time.

"I'll have to go back to the office and get some more," Willoughby was grumbling. "A complete waste of half an hour at least."

"Couldn't I go for you, sir? I've my evening rounds all made, and . . ."

Willoughby hesitated, then reached in his coat pocket and brought out some keys. "Why, yes, Harvey, that's a good idea. I have to see a patient at the College Hospital anyway, and I'll walk over there while I wait. The car is right down in the parking lot, license 4D622. Here's the key and here's the key to the office. You'll find the bottle on the top shelf of the medicine cabinet in the treatment room. Be a little careful at the corners. The front tires are worn."

It was beginning to drizzle as he left the long building, but Cyrus was glad to be out. It would be good to drive a car even the couple of miles downtown and back again, good to be out of the hospital smell for even twenty minutes or so. Not that you minded it when you were here. You got too used to it for that. But sometimes on a damp fresh night like tonight you noticed when it wasn't there and it was good. Maybe driving along he'd be able to figure something out. Willoughby wasn't acting what you'd call guilty, not that you'd know how guilty people would act, as a matter of fact, until you'd seen a couple. But it stood to reason their reaction time would be a little different or something, and Willoughby's certainly didn't seem to be. Even his annoyance had come with hair-trigger normalcy.

He got in the car and backed it out of the parking place and headed toward the gate. Gosh, they kept these grounds dark. One way of saving money, probably an order from the mayor, but if a patient got loose it would be damn easy to run over him before you knew it. He grinned at the gate keeper as he drove through. Fun driving a car like this, fun to be successful and have a big car and a big practice and a lot of prestige, or would it be? Sure it would. Probably once you got it you couldn't get along without it. But would a man murder to keep it, suppose someone knew something that could take it away? Well, some people might. Willoughby? Everett? Gosh, you wouldn't think so.

Wonder how the Pepper kid is making out. Talk about your orchids with steel inner springs. Talk about your casual crust. Watch your step with that kid, Hard Boiled, he told himself as he felt a dangerous softening somewhere inside. Watch your step.

That success you're talking about is a hell of a long way off. Even just plain eating, once you get out of here, is far enough away.

He was parking the car in front of Willoughby's office and opening the door beside the driver's seat. He swung his long legs onto the street. He'd been down here a couple of times with the old boy seeing him work his new wired-for-sound electrocardiograph, and wasn't that a honey of an instrument. He went up the steps, opened the door without any trouble, and made his way directly to the treatment room. He slipped the bottle in his pocket, went out to the car again and opened the door near the curb and started to slip across to the wheel. Something was in the way, Oh, Willoughby's bag, of course. Willoughby's bag?

A doctor could just drop the bottle in his bag. It was as if someone had suddenly shouted the words in his ear. He slipped across under the wheel and without stopping to think pulled the bag up on the seat beside him and unfastened the strap that held it. Then he was peering into it with his pocket flashlight. Cripes, doctors carried around a lot of stuff; blood-pressure thing there in that leather case, ophthalmoscope, hypodermics, and then all the bottles and stuff here in the side pocket. You'd think Willoughby would be the kind of guy to keep them all in neat little straps in labeled rows, but here they

154

were all in a heap. He pulled out the top ones and peered at them by the dash light. Metaphen. Alcohol. Codein. Whoa now, insulin. Doctors didn't usually carry insulin around with them; they could, of course, but patients usually had their own. Crystalline insulin too. The bottle looked damn familiar. Well and it would. All bottles of one brand were exactly alike.

Not exactly. Mechanically and almost unwillingly he turned the bottle on its side and peered at the control number, and something died inside of him. Oh, hell, it couldn't be that. But there were the numbers, 94459, little red numbers dancing in front of his eyes. Maybe he was seeing things this time. He switched on his pocket light again to reinforce the faint glow from the dash. Nope, there they were, 94459.

He dropped the bottle in his pocket, carefully fastened the strap of the bag and started the car. So what? Confront Willoughby and have him look blank or smile that amused smile of his? So what else? Tell Everett and have Everett call Bowman and tell him to put him in a tepid bath in Psycho till his brain cleared. So what else exactly? Anyone could have put that bottle in Willoughby's bag. His car was often out in front of the hospital, and his bag was pretty apt to be in the car. It would be a smart way of getting rid of it. But still, here was the bottle, and that it was the bottle that he'd given himself the entirely ineffective shot from two nights before, he hadn't now any doubt whatever.

He was driving automatically back toward the hospital, the windshield wiper going to clear away the drizzle, his wheels making a swish-swish as they went along the wet streets. Willoughby would never have left that bottle in his bag. But maybe he just hadn't had time to get rid of it. Maybe . . . Oh, what a hell of a mess! Maybe Cutter was right and he ought to have left the damn thing alone. Maybe Willoughby had good and plenty reason to do away with that Faine female. Undoubtedly he had. He was entering the hospital gates. So what? Well, first thing tell Sally. She was going to meet him in the interns' library, a hell of a plushy place but the only place you could entertain women, and what a place for a meeting to discuss murder. Wonder if she'd be back by now. Gosh, it was dark along these drives, especially in this fog. All he could see was the dimly lit buildings.

He passed the interns' home and curved around toward the parking place. His lights made a clear path along the drive that ended abruptly in darkness, but just on the edge of that darkness he saw a figure hurrying along the walk toward him, toward the interns' home. He could only dimly see it but there was something about the carriage, the way it moved. Sally. His heart gave a little jump and he started to put on the brakes and hail her.

XVI

IT was almost dark as Sally maneuvered her car out the muddy stony drive of Barehill Farm and onto the main road. It was beginning to drizzle and the twenty miles back to town seemed an awfully long way to go alone, especially when you were so full of information. She was hungry too, she suddenly realized. Mrs. Hillsley must have had supper very early because there had been no sign of food in the over two hours she had spent there. She balanced the urge for a cup of coffee against the urge to spill her news and the coffee won.

Quite properly too, she realized when she was sitting before it at a counter a few minutes later and ordering a hamburger and then lemon pie, for food was food, and all this information she'd dragged out of Maggie Hillsley, however fascinating, didn't, when you got right down to it, point very conclusively toward any one person who might have murdered Miss Faine.

The woman had had an illegitimate child, a spicy morsel if you will, but scarcely grounds for murder, except on the part of the child, and this particular child seemed to have been sufficiently buffaloed by her erring mother to have believed the erring mother was a martyr. Well, maybe she was. That might give whoever might have been the father grounds for murder, supposing Miss Faine had been harboring a grudge all these years and was just waiting to spill the scandal. But spilling the scandal about the father would spill it about herself too, and that wouldn't seem to go along with Caroline Faine's overdeveloped instinct for self-preservation.

Start from another tack. The woman had had an illegitimate child and Willoughby had delivered it. Why? Well, either Willoughby himself was the father, but Mrs. Hillsley had been pretty sure he wasn't and she'd been in a position to observe and seemed good at it too, or else Miss Faine had had some sort of hold on him. That would explain his altruism and might also give him a motive for murdering her now. If it wasn't either of those it was pure Galahad. It hardly made sense that a man would go to all that trouble to help a woman and then turn around

158

twenty years later and murder her. Or did it? Wouldn't that depend on why he'd helped her in the first place? Cyrus would know more about that than she did.

Who else now? De Grasse? It sounded as if all de Grasse had done was not come across with a marriage Miss Faine had been expecting to put over. Could he have been the father and promised to marry her after it was all over and then balked? In that case he might have murdered her now to keep her from spilling the scandal. Perhaps she'd been blackmailing him for years. But the way Mrs. Hillsley talked, it was more as if Miss Faine had been trying to keep the baby a secret from de Grasse. Sally brought up a picture of the fat, ruddy, stupid-looking doctor. He must have changed a lot or had an awful lot of money to have ever had any charm even for someone as unpredictable as Miss Faine. It hardly seemed as if he could have got very far with her short of marriage. Well, ask Cy about that too.

And where did Dr. Everett fit in? Mrs. Hillsley hadn't known anything about him, which was more relief than Sally had realized it would be, but there were those interdepartmental memos. If they meant what they seemed to imply, why wasn't Everett ever around during all the time Miss Faine was at Barehill Farm? Maybe all they meant was just what she had first believed, just a couple of casual dates which happened to get official attention. Now Sally brought up a picture of the spunky little superintendent. He was kind of small. Could he ever have had any attraction for a woman like Miss Faine? Maybe. There was an awful lot of force in that short frame, a lot of charm too. But what would have been her charm for him? And even granting the charm, which was difficult, you just couldn't see as square a guy as that in the role of seducer and abandoner of women.

Of course people changed a lot in twenty years, she told herself carefully as she polished off her pie and started out to the car again. It was pretty hard to visualize what any of those people might have been like when they were young. Young? Young like Cy and herself? Miss Faine, for instance. Miss Faine must have had an awful lot of the old oomph. She couldn't have, but she obviously must have with all these men in her life. Maybe Dr. Everett was a reformed rake. Maybe Dr. de Grasse in his twenties had been one of those hearty football people that so many gals were pushovers for. Maybe Dr. Willoughby had been the literary type that made time while he was murmuring Shakespeare in your ear. You couldn't tell. You couldn't know, now. All you could know was that Caroline Faine, whatever her lure was, had got around quite a bit with the boys, but had never been what could be called a sweet or charming little woman, that is unless Mrs. Hillsley's tale was entirely false. And one thing Sally was somehow sure of was that Mrs. Hillsley's tale was not entirely false.

It was dark when she got on the road again and she had to strain continually through the dampness to see her way, but it didn't stop her stream of thought. How much had Kenny known? Had she known about Evelyn? Of course she had, but how much else did she know? Gosh, loyalty was a funny thing. Maybe you didn't run into it often between women, but when you did . . .

Did Evelyn know that Kenny knew? How much did Evelyn know, as a matter of fact? Did she know herself who her father was? Was Mrs. Hillsley right that Miss Faine had told her the whole story and worked on her sympathies? Of course she was. Sally suddenly saw the pale frightened girl with her hand up to her cheek. No wonder she had been afraid of everybody, no wonder she had had this violent hatred of all men. But was there one man whom she was especially violent against? Everett, she had to admit unwillingly. That might just as well mean he had done something cruel to her father as anything else, or to Miss Faine herself. There seemed no way to fit Everett into the picture and keep his feet clean. Of course Cyrus had said Evelyn had flared up at Willoughby too when Miss Faine died. Maybe her attitude toward Everett didn't mean anything after all.

The change in Evelyn still wasn't explained by anything she knew, yet, or didn't seem to be. Unless —unless Evelyn was the guilty one. But guilt didn't make a person bloom, even guilt that was hopelessly bound up with relief. No, the clue lay in Evelyn's father. Her father? She didn't look like Miss Faine and so—and so she ought to look like her father. Sally tried as hard as she could to bring up a clear picture of Evelyn's face and to fix the features in her mind, but it was so blurred with that composite picture of strain and relaxation, of grimness and softness, that all she could see was the dark burning eyes like Miss Faine's, but not exactly like Miss Faine's, warmer, softer, and not so black. Who else had eyes like that? She almost knew. She could see them with a sort of masculine aura around them but she couldn't make the rest of the man's face come into focus.

It wasn't such a long drive after all. Here she was already back in the city. The eyes of Evelyn Moore were dancing in front of her. She would have to go to Evelyn and try to make her realize it was to her interest to talk. Perhaps if she could get her to listen to what Mrs. Hillsley had said, perhaps if she could get her to realize that she had been nursing a devotion to something pretty low and frightful all these years . . . Undoubtedly Miss Faine had been building on Evelyn's fear of being called a bastard. But heavens, bastards, oh, call them love children, a lot more romantic word, were almost socially correct these days. If that was all that made Evelyn so afraid of being attractive to men . . . If she could just get Evelyn to talk, if she could just figure out whose eyes were like those of Evelyn's . . . She was parking the car now. She'd hurry to the interns' home and put in a call for Cy and wait in the parlor and think.

As she got out of the car another pair of eyes suddenly came before her mind, like Miss Faine's, dark and intense, but warmer, kinder. She could see the face that went with the eyes. Oh, it couldn't be that, but it must be. Wait, just wait till she could tell Cy. She was hurrying along the walk. Heavens, it was dark. All you could see when a car came in the gate was its lights. The drizzle was rather nice except that it made seeing pretty difficult. She paused to avoid the approaching car and felt someone or something suddenly close behind her. She tried to step back, but something back there in the dark wouldn't let her, wouldn't even let her stand still. She tried with all her might to resist it, but she couldn't. She felt herself falling right into that path of brilliant light, and then the path of light was on top of her beating her down.

XVII

EVERYTHING was all confused. It was queer this way, dreaming two dreams at once, that awful one of seeing Cyrus in the car—what was he doing in a car anyway, especially a big ritzy one like that—seeing him and waving to him and then feeling this sharp compulsion, feeling herself falling, falling right in front of it. Dreaming that, and at the same time seeing his face right in front of her, looking the way she had always wanted it to look, not hard-boiled and flippant, not detached and medical at all. She stirred uneasily and something hurt, so she lay still again but this was too pleasant a dream to let slip. She kept her eyes on Cyrus' face. He was talking, murmuring something over and over.

"Gosh, kid, gosh, I'm glad to see those eyes again.

I ran you down, Sally. You must have slipped or something and fallen right under the wheel. I swerved as hard as I could, but I still hit you. I don't see how it happened, baby, because I saw you. I was slowing down to hail you, and then there you were in the road, and there I was socking you. Don't close your eyes, Sally, keep looking at me. Are you all right, kid?"

And this was very pleasant, but he was trying to say something, something about hitting her, about her slipping. But she didn't slip. There had been that compulsion, that something behind her, driving her, pushing her. Pushing. That was it. Somebody had pushed her. Tell Cy and make him feel better. This was lovely, this looking at him, this having him look at her like this, but it wasn't fair.

She stirred again and started to say, "Slipped nothing, I was pushed, big boy," when her eyes drifted beyond him. There were a lot of faces there beyond him. Dr. Cutter and Dr. Everett and Dr. Willoughby and Miss Wiley. If she was pushed, somebody must have pushed her. Somebody? Somebody who didn't want her to tell about Tod's Corner. Her mind was perfectly clear for a moment. Maybe one of these people didn't want her to tell about Tod's Corner. Maybe the person who had pushed her was right here in the room and he mustn't know, yet, that she knew what had happened. She had got as far as *Slipped*

165

nothing. I— when her labored mental processes reached that conclusion. She stopped abruptly, and shut her eyes.

She could hear somebody saying, "She's fainted again. Will you all go out, please. She'll come to in a moment but I'm afraid so many people . . ." She kept her eyes resolutely shut until the room was very still again, then opened them cautiously. It was only Dora Cutter bending over her, a poor substitute for the hard-boiled guy, but there weren't those other frightening faces beyond. She opened them wider.

"We're calling your father," Dora Cutter was saying gently and soothingly. "He'll be here very soon." And what was the point of that?

"I don't want my father," she said. "I want Cyrus Harvey."

She could see the resident hesitating. "I've got to see him," she said. "I've got to see him right away and alone."

Dora Cutter hesitated a moment longer. "All right," she said quietly then, and in a moment there was Cyrus bending over her again with the same marvelous look in his eyes. But Dr. Cutter was still there and she couldn't talk with Dr. Cutter there, because it might be anybody, anybody but Cyrus. Her eyes went to Dora Cutter and back to Cyrus and he wasn't so dumb because his mouth twisted into a half

166

grin and he got up. "I guess maybe you aren't wanted, old girl," he said mockingly to Dora Cutter. "Don't you sense that, and you a psychiatrist?"

Sally's heart twisted a little at his words. He was laughing at her. Maybe that anguished look had been just remorse. Maybe he and Dr. Cutter . . . She heard the door close, and shut her eyes again. Lord, she felt terrible. And then somebody, and she didn't have to open her eyes to know who, somebody was on the bed beside her holding her tight and shaking with a long almost hysterical shudder, his face buried in her hair.

She felt so fine after a moment that she was able to say with nearly normal flippancy, "This isn't what I wanted to be alone with you for, my lad. Look, where was Cutter half an hour ago? No, I'm not crazy, or delirious," as she saw the worried look come creeping back into his eyes. "The thing is, I didn't slip and fall in front of that car you were driving, Cy. I was shoved."

"You were—shoved?"

"That's right, shoved, by someone's hands. I could feel them, Cy, and I thought if Cutter was here on the ward, why . . ."

He looked at her, then shut his eyes for a minute, then he was on the bed holding onto her again, but only for a moment this time. Then he got up and remarked with great obtuseness, "I'm sorry, kid, but if you knew what I've been through since that car hit you . . ."

"Don't mention it," she said ironically, and watched him as he picked up the bell from the head of her bed and deliberately rang it.

"Miss Pepper would like some ice water," he said when the nurse appeared, and then chattily, "she's feeling much better. Lucky break for us that Dr. Cutter happened to be right up here. Had she been here long?"

"Oh, yes," the nurse was clearly delighted at this sociability on the part of hard-boiled Dr. Harvey. "She's been working all evening on an appendicitis in the ward. little Miss Kleber from Women's Medical. Perhaps you knew her."

"I don't think so." Cyrus' burst of chattiness vanished as quickly as it had come and the nurse disappeared with a bewildered frown.

"Well," he said, turning back to Sally, "that's that. Maybe if you're going to live we'll be glad of that murderous push. It oughtn't to be too hard to find out where several people were half an hour ago, and if we can . . ." He broke off. "Willoughby," he said slowly, "was right around somewhere damn convenient, unless he was still at the College Hospital, and I can find that out. Know a guy on Willoughby's service over there. Everett . . ." He shrugged. "Evelyn . . ."

"Evelyn," said Sally with an effort because she felt her head was going to blow up and scatter her hair all around the room at any moment, and because she wanted to get the information out before anything so unpleasant happened, "Evelyn was at a concert with Henry Bowman, at least I think she was, Cy." It seemed hard to keep her mind on the subject. It was important to tell him but there was so much to tell. "Cy, what are all those people doing outside, Dr. Everett and Dr. Willoughby and all?"

"Those"—Cyrus' grin turned sardonic again— "oh, I called them. Nice hour I've had since I drove gaily into the grounds and on top of you. Bringing you up here expecting you to stop breathing any moment, then Cutter reminding me that since it was Willoughby's car and I was on an errand for him I'd better let him know, and since Dr. Everett was in charge of the hospital and more or less in charge of me, I'd better let him know. It never occurred to me they'd come right over to view the body, but I keep forgetting you're the daughter of the president of the Schuylkill Bank and one of our more important hospital trustees. I didn't remember it until someone said 'Better call her father," in a sort of hushed and reverent voice. I realized then why everybody was

169

looking at me as if they were thinking, 'Criminal negligence, just the kind of irresponsible, hairbrained stunt Harvey would pull.' I hadn't realized it before probably because"—he frowned down at her —"I was kind of preoccupied with you, kid. Look, did you find anything out?"

"Did I find anything out? I'm exploding. You'll never believe it, Cy, but . . ."

There was a knock at the door and the nurse slipped in with the pitcher of water.

"Thanks," said Cyrus politely. "Will you ask Dr. Cutter to come in?" When the nurse disappeared again, he said, "If you're going to be laid up, I'm going to need help, and if Cutter's cleared she'll be damn useful. Do you mind, kid?"

"Of course not." Sally found she really didn't, and that was funny. It must have been that wordless interlude on the bed. Not that he'd said anything, but some things didn't need saying. "Though I'm not going to be laid up," she added indignantly and hoped her head wasn't going to explode before Dora Cutter got there.

"Hello, Cutter," Cyrus was smoking the inevitable slightly squashed cigarette when the resident stuck her head inquiringly in the door. "Sally's going to live, I guess. We're glad to hear you've been busy on the ward here for the last hour. You ought to be glad too, old girl. What the kid wanted to murmur in my ear, Cutter, was that she didn't slip under that car I was driving, she was pushed—by whoever murdered Caroline Faine, I suppose."

Dora's serene face hardly changed, but her eyes widened slightly. "But why?" she said, "why, Sally?"

"She was on her way back to spill an earful. She'd been detecting, that's why."

"Couldn't you see who it was?" Dora said with great practicality.

"Well, I wasn't expecting to be pushed," said Sally almost indignantly, "and it's dark as the bottom of a treacle well out there. I saw the lights of the car and then well, somebody shoved me."

"We know, kid. You don't need to prove it. I've been expecting something like that to happen, only I hoped it wouldn't be to you." He shrugged. "We thought maybe you as the only non-scoffer in the hospital, Cutter, would like to sit in on this . . ."

"I would." Dora sat down and folded her hands. "Do you feel able to tell us about it, Sally?"

"No," said Sally, "but I feel less able not to. Oh, gosh," she heard a deep authoritative voice in the hall "That's Dad. Look, Dr. Cutter," her eyes were darkly imploring, "he'll want to move me somewhere more elegant, but you tell him I can't be moved. I won't leave this place right in the midst of everything. I won't. Please, Dr. Cutter."

A big burly figure appeared in the door. "Hello,

Dad," she said brightly. "I hope Mother isn't worried. It's those darn high heels you're always growling about. I slipped right in front of Dr. Willoughby's car and almost wrecked it. You'll be lucky if he doesn't sue."

"We're lucky you aren't dead, working around this slum spot. Always knew it was a fool idea, always knew something would happen. Well, we'll have to move you somewhere decent right away."

Sally glanced at Dora Cutter and as the resident spoke with soft politeness, "I really think she'd better, not be moved for a day or so. There doesn't seem to be any concussion, but she ought to lie perfectly quiet. I'm sure Dr. Willoughby will agree," she smiled as wanly as she could.

It would be fun to see Dad's face if he knew the trouble she was really dabbling in, fun but scarcely worth it right now. And as for the trouble she was planning for herself for life, well, that was a bridge to cross when you came to it. But the main thing had always been to find someone who never bored you, and it looked very much as if she had. If Dora would only hurry and get rid of that bank president she had for a father before she got too sleepy to tell what had happened to her, everything would be all right.

It was a long time. Dr. Willoughby had to come in and reassure Mr. Pepper about Sally's condition. Dr. Everett had to come in and reassure Mr. Pepper about the condition of the hospital and Miss Wiley had to come in and reassure Mr. Pepper about the condition of the food Sally was likely to get. And all of them gave the impression, as Cyrus had said, that in their hearts they knew he had run Sally down out of sheer animal exuberance and Sally was simply being a heroine and covering it up. It was all she could do several times not to shout out, "Somebody pushed me, I tell you. Somebody was trying to kill me. Was it you or you or you?"

It was a good half hour before she could settle down again and say, "Look, both of you, try and think who Evelyn Moore looks like because somebody around this hospital is her father and I think I know who. Her mother? Listen, kiddies, are we a bunch of Simple Susans!"

XVIII

CYRUS didn't know as he dragged his long legs one after another down the corridor a half hour later whether he was too excited ever to sleep again or too tired to be excited about anything.

It had been a full evening, full and instructive, too damn instructive, in a good many ways. That insulin bottle, for instance, the one that had mysteriously disappeared from the lab icebox and just as mysteriously reappeared an hour or so ago in Dr. Willoughby's bag. Mysteriously reappeared? Well, if it wasn't mysterious it was painfully simple. Cyrus didn't like to think about that but he had to. Willoughby, Willoughby's bag. And Willoughby seemed to have been all tied up with Miss Faine and her little

174

interlude at Tod's Corner. Lord, what an investigator that Sally infant had turned out to be. Social Service had something if it could equip you to dig out information like this as casually as Sally seemed to have. Or else it was Sally that had something. Well, no doubt about that. He turned his mind deliberately away from Sally.

And Willoughby had been Miss Faine's doctor when she died. He could have switched the bottles easily enough, none easier except Evelyn Moore. And yet . . . Oh, hell, murder wasn't in Willoughby's character, not that kind of murder. Besides, there was the little matter of Sally and her stumble tonight that wasn't a stumble. Chances were almost a hundred to one that the person who had murdered Miss Faine had tried to murder Sally. And it wasn't Willoughby who had tried to murder Sally. Oh, it could have been. Willoughby knew that Cyrus had his car out. He didn't know that Sally had gone out to Tod's Corner, of course, unless he'd done some pretty elaborate snooping. Cyrus thought of the dark corridor outside the Record Room the night before. Hell, it must have been longer ago than that but it wasn't. Somebody, anyway, had done some pretty elaborate snooping, because somebody was waiting around for Sally to come back from Tod's Corner. And it might have been Willoughby. But the hitch was that Willoughby's intern over at the College Hospital around the corner seemed to be pretty sure he was still over there seeing a private patient about the time Sally was pushed.

Quarter of ten it had been, when he left Willoughby's office. Cyrus knew because he'd timed himself down and planned to time himself back just for the hell of it, just to see how fast you could make it in a big powerful car. It had been twelve minutes going down and he'd probably done a little better getting back. And Bill Pottle seemed pretty sure Willoughby hadn't left the College Hospital till after ten.

Cyrus grinned faintly as he remembered his telephone call. "Hello, College Hospital? Dr. Pottle, please. Hello, Bill, this is Cy. Willoughby still there? I'm trailing him. When'd he leave? More than an hour ago? Hell, he ought to be here then if he's ever coming." Sally and Dora listening almost breathless as he acted the dumb little act. "Any idea what time he left? What? Too bad about you and Mr. Swing. Well, thanks fella, go back to your radio."

"Praise the Lord for Raymond Gram Swing," he had murmured with relief as he laid down the phone. "Bill was griped as hell because Willoughby didn't leave in time for him to get back to hear the latest international comments. And I must have socked you before ten, Sally, so Willoughby's out." Sally had

176

beamed, "Cy, you sound just like a detective," and Dora had smiled that dry smile of hers and said, "Why shouldn't he?" Nice gals, both of them, and the nicer of them was his, though he hadn't got around to mentioning it to her yet. He pulled his mind back to business again.

So everything pointed to Willoughby's murdering Miss Faine and everything pointed away from his trying to murder Sally, and that was no help at all. But there was this bottle sitting in his pocket. He felt to make sure it was there and it was. You weren't going to get any further by just carrying it around and straining your mind in silence. There was one thing you could do. If Willoughby was still with that pneumonia patient, which was where you ought to have been all this time, you could up and show it to him. He probably wasn't, but you could see. He headed toward the cross wing marked Medical and turned in at the men's side.

"Dr. Willoughby still here?"

"Yes, and I wish he'd go home," the night nurse yawned luxuriously. "He's been waiting around to see how that pneumonia's going to stand the bigger dose. Just putting on his things—I hope. He said"— she looked almost awake for a moment—"you were rather preoccupied with a near homicide. What'd he mean?"

"I was"—Cyrus didn't bother to explain—"but looks like it's not going to hang me." He turned into the office marked Doctor. His hand was on the bottle and there was a sinking feeling in his stomach. "Dr. Willoughby?"

"Oh, hello, Harvey. Too bad about Miss Pepper," the chief seemed normally friendly and nothing more. "You must be relieved that she wasn't seriously hurt."

"Well, kind of," Cyrus tried to grin. "I'm sorry I didn't get over sooner, but it seemed the least I could do was to stick around and see if I could be any help. How is the man?" He was stalling for time. How was he going to go about this? What was Willoughby going to say when he did?

"Not too good"—the chief was shrugging into his coat—"but there's nothing to do but wait and see." He reached for his hat.

"Dr. Willoughby." This time Cyrus did bring out the bottle. "I probably should have told you before, but when I went up to see Foster about that insulin test the other morning I found he'd done the test from a different bottle. Somebody had changed them, sir. The bottle I took from Miss Faine's room had the control number 94459. I noticed it because it was a telephone number I use rather often. The bottle Foster did the test from had a different number."

"That's very interesting, Harvey." The chief

sounded tired. "But why are you telling me all about it now?"

"Because I just found the original bottle, Dr. Willoughby. See the number here, 94459."

"Really." Willoughby still sounded only mildly interested. "Where did you find it?"

"In your bag, sir. In your car. I've no excuse to offer for having found it, but I did and I thought you ought to know."

"In my . . ." Willoughby broke off. "Let me see that bottle, Harvey." He held out his hand and Cyrus a little unwillingly placed the precious glass object in it. Willoughby studied it or seemed to study it for a long moment, then he looked directly at Cyrus. "Perhaps I should ask why you were looking in my bag, Harvey," he said drily, "but instead I think I'll tell you that I have never seen this bottle before. Frankly, I was never sure till this minute that it existed except in your mind." He smiled a little. "You really have been going into this affair, haven't you," he said. "I'm beginning to think you may have something to go into."

"Yes, sir," said Cyrus politely. "I'm beginning to think you may have always thought so. Sally Pepper was out at Tod's Corner this evening, talking to a Mrs. Hillsley. There seem to have been quite a few things connected with Miss Faine that quite a lot of people wouldn't have wanted to come out. Somebody even wanted to keep them quiet to the extent of trying to murder Sally this evening, Dr. Willoughby. She didn't slip under your car, sir, she was pushed."

"Pushed," Dr. Willoughby raised his eyebrows. "It did seem rather strange to me that she could have slipped. Did you see anyone behind her, Harvey?"

"No, but she was practically out of the range of headlights herself. I only recognized her because, well, I sort of recognized her walk even in the half dark. I couldn't see beyond her at all. But she wasn't mistaken, sir. Sally isn't the sort of girl to imagine a thing like that."

"I don't believe she is, especially in the light of this bottle." Willoughby looked down at it again and then straight at Cyrus. "I'd like to give you my assurance, Harvey, that I had nothing to do with pushing Miss Pepper under my own car. That is, if you need it."

"I don't." Cyrus grinned wearily. "Pottle over at the College Hospital tells me you were over there when the thing happened. You made him miss Raymond Gram Swing, sir."

Willoughby grinned too for a second. "The research mind," he murmured, "leaves nothing open to question. Good work, Harvey."

"I didn't really think you had." Cyrus was faintly apologetic. "But . . ."

"Perhaps I'm the one that should be apologetic,"

180

interrupted Willoughby. "I didn't really believe there had been a murder, till now. One's mind doesn't run along those lines unless one is very young and elastic. There was that old unfortunate matter Miss Pepper seems to have run into, but it was pretty much of a closed book—I thought. Evidently"—he weighed the bottle in his hand—"it isn't. I wonder," his voice hardened, "who would have thought my bag was a good place to get rid of this bottle. I think I'll try to find out, if you don't mind, Harvey. Suppose you let me keep the bottle for a day or so and we'll see what's what." He looked at Cyrus inquiringly. "You can imagine that I am as anxious to have this thing cleared up quickly as you are, now that there's no question of its existence. The talk that is going around is not a help to one's professional reputation."

Cyrus looked at the bottle lying in his chief's hand and had an impulse to snatch it back. He had had so much trouble over that bit of evidence. Even though it was evidence supported by nothing but his own word, he somehow wanted to hold onto it. Yet what could he do with it? While Willoughby might show it to Everett and—Everett? Well, that would be one way of bringing things to a head.

"All right, sir," he said. "I'm glad to have you working with me at last. My reputation is taking quite a beating over this thing too, you know."

"I've always enjoyed working with you, Harvey."

The chief smiled warmly. "Let me know if anything new comes up with that pneumonia."

"I will, sir," said Cyrus. He was tired and confused but as he left his chief in the court and started over to the interns' home he had a definite conviction that Willoughby was neither Evelyn Moore's father nor Caroline Faine's murderer. It just didn't add up that way. As for how it did add up, oh, well, get to bed. He was going to need a clear mind tomorrow, especially if this hunch of his that another twenty-four hours would show some daylight meant anything. Maybe when he saw it he'd wish he hadn't, but facts were facts.

One thing still to do, though, before he hit that bed. He was yawning, but he didn't turn into his own room when he came to it. He went two doors beyond. "Hello, Henry, still up?" He perched on the desk and pulled out a cigarette.

Henry Bowman looked up from a book he was reading in bed. "Hello," he said. "I always read a little before I go to sleep."

"Thought you'd still be out. Hear you took the Moore kid to a concert tonight. Have fun?"

"Why, yes, she seemed to enjoy it."

"Just get home?" Cyrus was completely casual, but such curiosity was out of character. Bowman stiffened.

"Why, not so long ago. Though, as a matter of fact I don't see . . ."

"Where I get off to be asking so many questions." Cyrus grinned. "I just wanted to know where Evelyn was at say ten o'clock. I thought maybe you could tell me without my making a big fuss about it."

"It's not exactly your business, is it, Cy?" Bowman's voice was mild.

"Well, kind of. I'll tell you why if you'll tell me where she was."

Bowman looked at him, obviously making up his mind. "Ten o'clock?" he said at last. "Well, I'd say offhand that she was taking a deep breath just as the orchestra broke into the second movement of Beethoven's Fifth. I think she found it quite a release from all that strain she's been under," he added somewhat clinically. "I was glad I'd taken her."

"Pretty sure about the time?"

"Well, the concert was over at ten twenty-five. We came right home, but we walked. Evelyn wanted to, drizzle and all. I think that did her good too." He smiled softly as if remembering something.

Cyrus looked at him curiously. "Got it kind of bad, haven't you?" he remarked. "Well, I think that's nice, particularly as Evelyn was taking a deep breath of delight just as the orchestra broke into the second movement of something or other. You see, Henry, just as Evelyn was taking a deep breath, someone pushed Sally under a car I was driving, and it's nice to know it wasn't Evelyn. We aren't saying anything

183

until we have asked around. I'm only telling you because I think you have sense. Sally was on her way back from finding out some pretty important things about the past life of one Caroline Faine, things someone, we're still finding out who, might not want to have spread around."

Bowman put down his book and looked attentive. "Anything to do with Evelyn?" he said. "That girl interests me a good deal."

Cyrus grinned and wondered what Henry would say if he knew, wondered whether he would care. Well, it wasn't his business to tell him. If, by interested he meant *interested,* he'd find out soon enough. "Some." he said casually. "I guess I'm more interested in who killed Miss Caroline Faine."

"You're sure somebody did kill her?"

"Yep, especially after this push-push business."

Bowman stirred. "Well, Evelyn certainly didn't do any pushing tonight," he said, "and she couldn't have murdered her aunt, because she was almost fanatically devoted to her. She was telling me all about how that sadist of a woman sacrificed her whole life for her. It made me creep a little, she was so sincere. People never really know what other people are like, do they?"

Cyrus got up and threw his cigarette into a corner and left it burning there, grinning at Bowman's complete lack of interest in murder in the face of love.

184

"No," he said. "I don't think she murdered her aunt, but she might know something that would tell us who did."

"I'd wait awhile before I asked her a lot of questions," said Bowman. "She's still pretty much upset over the whole business."

"So's Sally," said Cyrus unfeelingly. "So, if you want to know, am I." He walked to his own room and fell into bed and slept.

XIX

THE fog and drizzle had cleared away during the night. Sun was streaming in the window of the kid clinic, but even if it had been raining hoptoads it would have looked like sunshine to Evelyn. Something inside her was swooping and soaring, and it was wrong to feel this way so soon after Aunt Caroline's death, wrong and horrible, but she kept right on feeling it.

"You're looking better this morning, Katie. The doctor will be ready for you in a minute, Jimmy. Have you been taking your medicine, Pete? Yes, of course it's going to make you better." The words came with cheerful warmth, and she felt warm and cheerful. She had probably never felt warmer toward the world in her life, but she didn't really know what she was saying because of the swooping.

Only twice reality broke through. Once when Miss Kenny said, as they stood holding the arms and legs of a struggling little colored boy while the intern extracted two dried peas from one nostril, "Sally Pepper's up in the Infirmary. Got herself knocked down by a car last night right here on the hospital grounds. Slipped or something, they tell me. Willoughby's car, and who do you think was driving it? The hard-boiled guy. Bet he's wanting to cut his throat."

Then she had a brief sharp vision of Sally Pepper brushing her hair, holding a mirror, smiling, to her face. Dr. Bowman had said, "Aren't you wearing your hair different or something?" And just thinking about it made the swooping deeper and stronger than ever. And now it was Miss Pepper who was in the Infirmary, Miss Pepper who had brushed her hair and held the mirror.

"Oh, Miss Kenny," she said with distress, "is she badly hurt?"

"Don't think so. Afraid of concussion for awhile, but looks like she was just shaken up. That's what Dr. Cutter up there says, anyway."

"Perhaps they'll let me see her this evening. She's been awfully nice to me." She wondered as she said

187

it if Sally Pepper's illness had anything to do with Dr. Cutter's asking her out to lunch today. She hadn't been able to think of any other reason, but then she hadn't been able to think much at all this morning.

The other time the present broke through was just as she was going off duty. She had seen a white duck figure coming down the corridor and it was funny, white duck was white duck, but she knew, even before she looked up at the face, even before the quiet voice said, "If you're going off duty won't you come have a sandwich with me somewhere?"

She looked up at him then, and wondered if that warm light in his eyes would go away if he knew—about her. It was crazy to think even for a minute that it wouldn't. It was crazy even to dream about it, and yet a piece of her mind kept right on dreaming.

"Dr. Cutter has asked me to have lunch with her," she said unhappily as they walked together across the course. "I'm just going to get dressed now." It was funny, Dr. Bowman didn't seem like a person who would get angry so easily, but he had looked terribly angry for a moment, though all he had said was, "Well, perhaps this evening then," and walked away.

Probably Dr. Cutter was just sorry for her, she thought when the woman doctor met her outside the nurses' home and began, in her light casual voice, to

188

tell her about Sally Pepper. Perhaps she was just try-ing to take her out of herself, as she had in the In-firmary when she was lying there in that dream-like state. It was queer, she had resented it then, had fought it bitterly, but now it didn't seem to matter. It was nice of Dr. Cutter but it didn't matter. Nobody needed to take care of her, nobody needed even to bother about her with this soaring feeling going on. Nobody? Well, almost nobody.

She scarcely listened to what the woman doctor was saying as they walked down to the corner tea shop and found a booth. Something about Miss Pep-per. Funny Miss Pepper should have been around the hospital in the evening. She was through work at five. Maybe Dr. Cutter was telling her why. She was saying something about Sally coming back from do-ing an errand somewhere, but it was hard to take time away from her own feelings to listen.

"How's if I crash this exclusive party?" She looked up in dismay. This wasn't the sort of place you'd expect Dr. Harvey to come, even if he did want to change from hospital food. Mike's was more his type. But here he was, and he was sitting down beside Dr. Cutter who was across from her, and Dr. Cutter looked glad to see him.

"I was just telling Evelyn," she was saying, "how you almost ran Sally down last night."

"Yeah," Dr. Harvey was pulling a cigarette from

189

a crumpled pack, but his eyes were on her face, and why should he look at her this way? "While you were at the concert, Evelyn. Bowman says you sat there like a little mouse listening to some symphony from before ten to almost ten-thirty."

"Yes," she drew in her breath. "It was lovely." But then she knew Dr. Cutter hadn't brought her here just out of kindness, and Dr. Harvey hadn't happened in, because his eyes were still on her face and they had a hard probing look and he was saying, "I'm sure glad you were at the concert with someone about then, Evelyn, because the reason I almost ran Sally Pepper down last night was she was pushed in front of the car by someone who figured I wouldn't be able to stop as quick as I did. And do you know where she was coming back from? You'll be interested in this, Evelyn. She'd just been out to see a relative of yours at Tod's Corner. Funny coincidence, wasn't it, her being pushed, just as she was coming back with some pretty surprising information about you."

She had a sudden feeling of something closing in on her. She might have known it was too good to be true. Aunt Caroline had always said she mustn't try to lead a normal life. She looked from one doctor to the other.

"Dr. Harvey doesn't want to frighten you, Evelyn, but he's terribly upset about Miss Pepper," Dr. Cutter was saying. It was a kind voice, but its kindness didn't make the trap any looser. It was the facts that were unkind. "He's sure you know something that could help us find out who did it," the kind voice was going on. "Because it must be the same person who murdered your—Miss Faine. Miss Pepper, you see, had just found out about—you, and we're wondering if perhaps the person who murdered your mother, wasn't—your father."

For the first time in over twenty-four hours she put her hand up to her cheek in the old defensive gesture. "No," she said. "No, please don't ask me about it. She wasn't murdered. She couldn't have been. She died of diebetes. Oh, you know she did, Dr. Harvey. You were right there."

"Sure she died of diabetes. But she wouldn't have, if she'd been getting any insulin. Someone kept switching the bottles so that all she was getting for about a week, with all those injections, was just water."

"Oh, but they couldn't have. I was right there, right with her all the time."

"I know you were," Cyrus put his elbows on the table and looked straight at her. "That's what makes it so funny your not wanting to admit the possibility of—murder. It makes it look sort of . . . Well, you can see for yourself who could have switched those bottles the easiest."

"Oh," there was horror in the girl's voice, "but she was my . . ."

"Sure, we know." Cyrus was unimpressed. Dora Cutter was watching her detachedly as if she were watching a play. "But it's happened before. The police wouldn't think that was proof that you couldn't have, you know."

"But why would I have wanted to? She'd sacrificed her whole life for me, to make up to me for what had happened. Why would I have wanted to?"

"Don't you know why?" This was Dora Cutter. She picked up her handbag and got out her compact with swift precision, and opened it and turned the mirror toward the frightened girl. "Look at yourself, Evelyn," she commanded. "Do you remember what you looked like a week ago? Look. Don't you look different, even to yourself?"

Evelyn pushed the mirror away. "I know," she whispered. "It's horrible of me to look like this. I can't help it. But I didn't murder her."

"What are you afraid of then?"

"What am I afraid of?" Her dark eyes grew darker and almost opaque for a moment. "Oh, if you only knew what it's been like, always. I'm afraid—of him."

"Who?"

She sat there stiffly silent.

"Do you think your father might have done it?"

192

She shook her head but there was fright and knowledge in her eyes.

"Who is your father? Don't you see how much more dangerous it is not to tell? If he got rid of your mother, the next step will probably be to get rid—of you."

She sat there her face and body stiff, and then suddenly she said almost expressionlessly, "Everyone thinks he's so wonderful. My mother used to laugh about it. It wasn't a nice laugh but how could it have been? He fooled everybody so completely. He even fooled her—twenty years ago. He ruined her life and he's ruined mine. What kind of a life can you have with no father, no name? That's why I was always afraid to speak to anyone or look at anyone for fear it might come out and make things harder than they already were for her and for me. But he didn't care. He just sat there behind that desk in that office pretending the only thing he cared about was the good of the hospital."

Cyrus' eyes had been fixed on her face. Now they moved for a fraction to Dora Cutter's as hers moved to meet his. A spark of comprehension passed between them, and then both pairs of eyes moved back to the girl's face.

"She did her best to make up to me for it," she went on. "She worked and became a success so that she could take care of me always. He didn't care, as long as it didn't touch him, but when she became superintendent of nurses they had a terrible quarrel. That was just before she became ill. That," she turned to Cyrus, "was what I thought for a while might have made her ill. She wanted him to do something for me. I don't know what, money or something, so that I could go away somewhere. I didn't want it, but she wanted it for me. She knew something disgraceful he had done when he was young and she threatened to expose him if he didn't. Oh"— she put her hand up to her face again—"I know it sounds horrible, but she was doing it for me."

"Did he do what she wanted?" Dora Cutter's voice might have been asking about the weather.

"No, but it was just then that she became so ill. If anyone killed her it must have been him. It must have. He'll probably kill me too, when he finds out I've told you all this."

"Sally said she thought you looked like Dr. Everett," said Cyrus carefully, "particularly your eyes."

"Yes," said the girl. "I know, that's part of what makes it so horrible." Then, as she saw another glance go between the two doctors, "Oh, why must you make me say all this? Why couldn't you just leave me alone? It wasn't so bad when nobody knew." She put both hands to her face and shook with silent sobs.

194

"It wasn't so bad when nobody had been killed," said Cyrus expressionlessly. "I thought Dr. Everett had a lot to do with this, but I wanted to be sure. I'm going to see him this afternoon, Evelyn, and I want you to come with me."

"Oh, I couldn't," she whispered. "I couldn't."

"And nobody has any right to try to make you." She hadn't heard steps, but there was someone beside her now. Now the trap was loosened. The somebody had sprung it and was protecting her from these two across the way. "I thought you'd be here," the voice was saying, and for all its quietness its impact was sharp and strong. "I tried Mike's first, then I knew you had to be here. I don't care who committed your lousy murder, Cy, if anyone did. You can't bully this kid. She's had enough without you're going third degree on her. You're going to leave her alone, see, and I'm here to see that you do."

She could feel the strong slender hands over her own, and she felt safe and almost happy.

Cyrus pulled himself out of the narrow seat and grinned down at the angry eyes behind the dark-rimmed glasses. "Keep your pants on, Henry," he said. "The bullying is all over, Evelyn is probably almost as swell a kid as you think she is. I can't lay off her entirely yet. We have to go pay a call, Evelyn and I. Will you, Evelyn? I'll call you at the nurses' home a little later. No one is going to hurt you. After this afternoon no one will ever hurt you again. Will you?"

"She won't. She can't. She's been through enough." Bowman's voice was possessive and protective. "He can't make you do anything you don't want to, Evelyn," but Evelyn took her hand gently from his and looked at him and smiled a wisp of a smile, then looked at Cyrus. It was as if this protective presence somehow gave her the strength not to need protection.

"I've been doing things I didn't want all my life," she said wearily. "I guess I can do one more, if it's to find out who murdered—my mother." At the last words her eyes met Bowman's squarely.

"Your mother," Bowman's hazel eyes glowed suddenly behind their glasses as if something had just brushed away a cobweb. "Miss Faine—your mother? So that was it?" He smiled unexpectedly. "God, you don't know what a relief it is to hear that bit of information. It makes you so much more—normal."

"Normal!" Evelyn almost gasped. "I was afraid you'd think . . . I thought you'd feel . . . Normal? Dr. Bowman?"

"Yes, your devotion and all. I tried to explain it on a compensation basis, and on a mother substitute fixation, but I didn't like explaining it that way. Your mother? Why, no wonder you've been the way you

196

have." His voice was warm and eager. "Oh, this is going to be a lot simpler than I thought."

Dora Cutter was getting to her feet with a faint smile on her face. "Come on, Cyrus," she said. "Psychoanalysis is always better managed in privacy."

"Give the kid something to eat, Henry." Cyrus pulled a crumpled dollar from his pocket and dropped it grandly on the table. "On me. We didn't seem to get around to it."

"And," he said when they were outside the door, "that passes the job of feeding me to you, old girl. That was my last buck. Got the price of a flock of hamburgers? I could use 'em." He was grinning, but it wasn't a very happy grin.

"Two flocks"—Dora Cutter tried to grin back— "with onion."

"And pickle," he blew out his breath wearily. "What a swell judge of character I turned out to be. The kid's right. Everett had us all eating out of his hand. I thought he was as good a guy as came."

"So did I, and I'm a psychologist."

"But that girl was telling the truth."

"Yes—as she saw it."

"No question Everett's her father?"

"I wouldn't think so."

"See anything else to do but put it up to him?"

"No, but it may not prove anything."

"Not if I went alone. Alone he'd just talk me down again. All in my mind, all another one of my fast ones. He'll have trouble talking Evelyn down. God, what a life that kid must have led. Of all the warped personalities."

"She's getting unwarped."

"Yeah . . . Kind of funny she should snap out of it quite so fast, hm?"

"Damn funny." The curse sounded odd in the woman's calm voice. "That's what makes me wonder a little about—Everett. Wish I could come along this afternoon."

"Wish you could."

"But I'd only be in the way."

"Yep"—he made a face—"looks like my show."

"Your show, yes, but look, Cy . . ." she hesitated. "Don't you shout Everett down, because I've an idea . . ."

"What?"

"Oh, nothing, but do a certain amount of listening."

"Hell, don't I?"

"It isn't exactly your role," she murmured. "Not that anybody would want it to be. How many hamburgers, six?"

XX

"WELL, Harvey?" The superintendent looked up from his desk with a smile that held no amusement and not much friendliness. There was a tray pushed to one side of his desk. The guy had been right, Cyrus thought inconsequentially, about the diet kitchen sending up more than he could eat, unless his appetite had fallen off very recently. Those sandwiches would look good if it weren't for the flock of hamburgers, but Everett didn't look likely to offer them to him today. When was it he was here before? Thursday, two days ago? Only two days, and he'd come then because Everett would be one person you could count on to see things straight and to act without pussyfooting.

He stood looking at the dynamic little man, and

199

tried to see him with new eyes, with the eyes of hate that had burned in Evelyn Moore's face when she was talking about him a couple of hours ago. Not only then. He had a quick clear vision of the girl looking across her aunt's bed at the little man. There had been hate in her eyes then, and he had wondered if it was specific or general. Well, he didn't wonder any more. Hate in Evelyn Moore's eyes, scorn in Miss Faine's eyes, scorn and triumph. Why had there been triumph? He blinked his eyes and kept looking at the man behind the desk, trying to visualize him as the source of all that malice, but all he saw in the face was the same energetic kindliness, the same tolerance of everything but injustice. It didn't look as if people's faces proved very much, because there were the facts.

It didn't occur to him, as he stood there, to be afraid. Even accepting the fact that he was probably face to face with someone capable of committing a murder, capable of attempting another, he still wasn't afraid because what could Everett do? He could get out a gun and shoot of course, but where would that get him? Everett might murder, but he'd never do anything just plain senseless. He stood there looking at the man he had known and admired for almost two years and wondered how to begin, and Dr. Everett stirred impatiently in his chair and re-

200

peated, "Well, Harvey," then added, "something new come up?"

"Yes, sir," said Cyrus slowly, "a good deal."

"About Miss Faine's death?" Everett smiled again and it was amazing how little warmth there could be in a smile. "Have you picked the culprit?"

"I don't know, sir." There was an ache in Cyrus' throat worse than anything since he had had his tonsils out. "That's what I have to talk to you about, but I realized there wasn't much good in talking to you by myself, because in a way, all I have still is ideas. I've lots of those, but it's pretty easy to brush aside ideas. I thought I'd better have someone on hand to hear what we were going to say to each other. And it sort of seemed as if the best person for that would be" —he went to the door and opened it—"your daughter, sir."

Everett half rose from his chair, but he didn't say anything. He just stood there looking at the girl with a tight, strained face.

"I've been having quite a talk about you with Miss Moore, sir," Cyrus went on with perfect courtesy. "From what she says you're about the only person around here with a really good motive for murdering Miss Faine and about the only person cold-blooded enough to do it. I found that hard to believe, Dr. Everett, but I'm beginning to realize

201

I'm not a very good judge of character. Miss Moore ought to know, I guess." He was silent, and the girl was silent by the door, waiting.

There was a long pause, and then Everett said almost as if he hadn't heard the charge. "Yes, she ought to know—a great many things she doesn't know now. I wonder how many of them she would be capable of believing after all the years of that rather special education she has had. Yes," he went on, looking up a little diffidently at the girl by the door, "I had plenty of motive for murdering Caroline Faine. She had taken away my happiness. I didn't know till a month ago just how completely she had done that. She had it in her power to take away my work too. She was very fond of power, Caroline Faine."

"Why wouldn't she be?" The words came from the doorway with suppressed violence. "It was all she had."

"It was all she wanted, my dear." Cyrus glanced at the girl to see how she would take that endearment. Her body and face were tense with bitterness, but it was hard to tell whether they had grown any tenser in the last few seconds. There was a limit, he realized, to the contracting power of muscles, and she must have reached that quite a few minutes ago.

"I discovered that, unhappily, some twenty years ago," Everett was going on in the same mild diffident voice. "And I've been watching her gather it and enjoy it ever since. It would have been psychologically interesting probably if it hadn't been so"—he smiled faintly—"painful."

"How can you say that?" Evelyn burst forth. "You were responsible for it all. You left her disillusioned and—with a responsibility. She did the best she could with what she had."

"Is that what she told you?" Everett smiled again but not with amusement. "I've wondered occasionally how she explained things. No, my dear, it was she who left me. It was inevitable that she would, of course, but you don't realize those things when you're in love. It was a shock, her turning from me, but what made it harder because I couldn't explain it was the bitterness that came afterwards. I never understood that bitterness till about a month ago. I never knew, till a month ago, that it was because of you that she missed up on a very promising marriage she had planned for herself. I, of course, was responsible for you, and I had nothing to offer her but honest love." His voice turned faintly sardonic for a moment. "I never knew till a month ago, you see, that you existed at all." He had been looking down at the desk as he talked. Now he looked up and straight at Evelyn Moore. "She must have enjoyed keeping that from me all these years. She was shrewd enough, and she knew me well enough—God knows she had had plenty of opportunity—to realize what that knowledge would have meant to me."

"I don't believe it," Evelyn's words came stiffly and automatically. "Stop him, Dr. Harvey. Stop him from saying these horrible things. They aren't true."

"Quite true, my dear." Everett didn't even look at Cyrus, his eyes were still on Evelyn. "I found them rather hard to believe myself at first. Except that she told me them in a rage, and people are apt to speak the truth in anger. I might never have known if it hadn't been for that temper of hers"—he smiled again and this time there was a flash of brutal amusement—"that and the will to power. I think she wanted to be directress of nurses chiefly because it would put her in direct conflict with me, she for the nurses, I for the interns and the hospital, give her a chance to dominate me again, though differently. What she forgot was that her only power over me had been emotional, and any emotion will die eventually. When she found that out over an absurdly minor point"—there was the sardonic smile again—"she was beside herself."

Cyrus stood absolutely still watching the changing expressions on the controlled face of the little man. Now it grew hard and cold. "She taunted me with—you, Evelyn. The fact that here you were and I could never have you. And that was intolerable, finding that I did after all have some link with the future and being refused the enjoyment of it. Twenty years was lost already, that was enough. I told her I was going to talk with you, ask you for at least a small share of your life, and it was then that she threatened me."

Cyrus could feel a tensing in his own muscles and wondered what Evelyn was feeling. It was coming now. Did Everett realize it was coming, or was it just the pent-up feelings of twenty years spilling over regardless of consequence. It didn't sound like it, as the little man went on calmly, patiently, as if he were trying to explain something difficult to a not-too-bright child.

"That was what was upsetting her just before"—he hesitated—"just before she became so ill. She did have a hold on me. Using it was going to hurt herself, but the temptation to use it was becoming irresistible. It was when I was a resident, you see, that Caroline and I—knew each other so well."

Cyrus felt his head nodding idiotically. Everything was slipping into place like one of those Chinese puzzles. An interdepartmental memo, *Will you kindly speak to your resident on Neurology about his attentions to student Caroline Faine,* flashed across his mind and dropped into place. An angry voice behind a door the first afternoon in the Nurses' Infirmary, *I tell you, Caroline, you can't do it,* that fitted into another differently shaped place near by.

Then there was another voice, the voice of a sick woman, but for all its weakness threatening and vindictive, *I'm not beaten, Les, Les, you'll see.* It hadn't occurred to him that what she was really saying was Bliss, Bliss, not until this precise minute. And she had been right, in a way. She had gone down but she was still busily dragging this basically decent little man after her. He pulled his mind back to what the basically decent little man was saying.

"I had very little money. Caroline was probably the most fascinating girl I had ever seen, and she wanted a great deal. Even then I had sense enough to realize that if I didn't provide it someone else would. I got the necessary money . . ." He looked at Cyrus and smiled, and suddenly it was a friendly smile. "You see," he said, parenthetically, "I am putting myself very much into your hands, Harvey, but they're probably as good hands as any.

"I got the money by selling liquor prescriptions. That must be hard to understand now. It was in a class then with, well not quite with illegal operations, but not far off. You are too young to remember Prohibition. A lot of ugly things came out of that social experiment and one of the ugliest was doctors who turned bootleggers. I was one of them for awhile, for the greater glory of glorious Caroline Faine." The words came out brutally. "I kept thinking if I gave her enough she might marry me. I should have known she never would. She left me for"—he shrugged—"that doesn't matter now." And, no, thought Cyrus mentally supplying de Grasse's name, that doesn't matter now. "But then, of course she didn't know there was going to be"—Everett turned directly to Evelyn—" you, my dear. You must have upset her plans a good deal, driving her away from her big chance to make a brilliant marriage, to the refuge of a mythical tuberculosis sanitarium. She was pretty sure of herself, Caroline. She evidently thought she could vanish completely for six months and then come back and start where she left off, but it didn't work that way. Her prospect married somebody else." He smiled a little cruelly.

"I didn't know any of this at the time, of course. When Caroline was through with a man, she was through. All I knew was that she was going around a lot with this other man, and suddenly disappeared for some time and then came back looking harder and more beautiful than ever. You're probably wondering why she didn't tell me about it and let me take the responsibility," he went on as Evelyn opened her mouth to speak. "But, you see, you never really knew Caroline Faine. That would, in a manner of speaking, have put her in my power, at the very least it would have put her under obligation to

207

me, besides making me quite unnecessarily happy. Neither of those prospects would have appealed to her.

"I don't think even the doctor who delivered her knew the baby was mine. He was another poor fish who was in love with her, more of a fish than I, for she never gave him anything even for a short time. If he did know, he undoubtedly thought, as you did"—he looked at Evelyn again—"that I was a black seducer. Technically, of course, I was, but hardly in spirit. I've always wondered about a certain hostility in that quarter. It's easy to understand now, but"—he shrugged—"it doesn't matter, of course.

"It's been a queer twenty years, so close officially to a woman who had been so important to you, watching your feelings shrink and harden and gradually, gradually crumble away. Then all of a sudden, at a bit of knowledge that earlier would have made your love limitless, to look inside you and find nothing but one hard little kernel—of hate. Yes," he said quite casually, "I had plenty of motive for murdering Caroline Faine. I thought of it a good deal in the last weeks before she died. But the real motive wasn't fear of what she could do to me, though she could undoubtedly have hurt my career a good deal. The real reason for my hate"—his eyes on Evelyn were almost shy for a moment—"was what she was doing to you, my dear."

Cyrus stirred uneasily as the superintendent stopped talking. He took out a pack of cigarettes and awkwardly shook one out and still more awkwardly lighted it. His eyes were on Everett's face. He heard a sound behind him and saw Evelyn moving toward the desk, moving slowly but steadily, almost as if hypnotized, until she stood directly in front of the little man whose warm, dark, burning eyes seemed to mirror her own.

"It can't be true," her low voice was murmuring. "It sounds true, but it can't be. I couldn't have been so wrong. I couldn't bear it if I had been that wrong all these years."

"I know," said Everett gently. "I felt that way too, once. But I did bear it. And," he added a little awkwardly, "I didn't have anyone to help me. You have, if you want help."

"But you . . ." she said wretchedly. "Oh, don't you see you're the one that's going to need help?" Suddenly she turned to Cyrus. "What are you going to do?"

"What do you think?" he muttered. "It's a lousy world, but you can't just shut your eyes to murder."

"Murder," Everett looked up with mild surprise. "You think—oh, no, Harvey. What I have been doing is settling an old score with"—he smiled that odd shy smile—"my daughter, not confessing to murder. Besides," he smiled at Harvey now, and there was enough power in him to make the smile faintly paternal, "I didn't know the fact of murder had been established in anybody's mind but your own."

"I'm afraid it's been established in quite a few minds, now, sir." Cyrus spoke miserably, but his blue eyes were attentive. "In Sally Pepper's for one. She has reason to be convinced, sir. She didn't slip and fall under that car I was driving last night. She was shoved, by someone who didn't want her to bring back all this information about Miss Faine and Evelyn." He paused. "Would you be able to tell me where you were at ten o'clock last night? It's none of my business, I know, any more than any of this is, but the police will probably think it's theirs."

"I was in my room," Everett spoke without hesitation. "You know yourself I was there when you called me. Is Miss Pepper sure about this? Isn't it possible she was just overwrought?"

"It was a half hour later when I got around to calling you, and I don't figure Sally Pepper as the overwrought kind. But that's just one thing, Dr. Everett. You remember that bottle I told you about, the one with the telephone number on it that disappeared? Well, somebody tried to get rid of it by putting it in Dr. Willoughby's bag. We found it last night."

"Who has the bottle now?" Everett sounded alert for a moment.

210

"Dr. Willoughby, sir. I think he's having it analyzed."

"I'll be interested to hear what he finds." Now Dr. Everett was noncommittal. "But even if it should turn out not to be insulin as you suspect, I hardly see how it gives you a case for murder. The whole complicated insulin story is your story with no other evidence to back it up except this you've just told me about Miss Pepper, and I think that sounds a good deal like the imaginings of a frightened girl. You can go to the police, of course, but I'd think it over pretty carefully first. There was a lot in Caroline Faine's life that could make a lot of people very unhappy if it came out into the open. You'll bring it out into the open, Harvey, if you go to the police, but I doubt if you'll prove a murder, and I don't see why you're so anxious to."

Cyrus could feel his mouth gaping idiotically. There was something almost ridiculous about this casual conversation with a more than probable murderer. Everett certainly had what it took. "Well," he said, "there is justice."

"Yes," Everett spaced his words significantly, "that's what I mean. There is justice."

Cyrus shut his mouth. "There's my own reputation for ordinary common sense and general integrity," he said, "though that's probably not vital, and then

211

there's Dr. Willoughby. If I have to choose between helping him clear his name and leaving a dangerous person at large, however much I may sympathize with that dangerous person in spots, well, I don't see that there's any choice. Maybe you had nothing to do with Miss Faine's death or Sally Pepper's accident, but if you didn't it ought to be awfully easy to prove that you didn't."

Everett looked suddenly exhausted. "You'll do what you think best, Harvey," he said faintly. "Go to the police, but I don't think you'll prove that I or anyone else murdered Caroline Faine."

Cyrus looked at him and then at Evelyn Moore She was looking at her father and then he was looking up at her and then their hands were touching across the desk. "I almost wish I weren't going to," he said slowly. "God knows I wish I didn't have to, but I do, and I am," and left them looking at each other.

XXI

EVELYN was lying on her bed looking at the ceiling. She had been lying there ever since she had come in a half hour ago. Her roommate, one of the student nurses on Surgical, was sitting across the room doing her nails. Every now and then she would cast a curious glance in Evelyn's direction and then go back to the exacting work of getting the forbidden fuschia on exactly right. In a little while it would be four o'clock and she would have to go back to duty, and if the polish wasn't dry by then it would be just too bad. She held up one hand and admired her work. Miss Faine would never have let you get away with a color like that. Better make the most of Miss Wiley while she was around. The next permanent directress would probably be another tough one. She

213

glanced at Evelyn again, and wondered phlegmatically how much there was to all those terrific rumors that had been going around since the directress died.

Nothing probably, but Evelyn had been kind of funny since that happened. Well, not exactly funny, except in not being as funny as she used to be. Mourning for somebody was supposed to make you all quiet and shut up inside, at least, the student considered, that was the way she had felt when her dog died. It was before, that Evelyn had acted as if she were in mourning. Now she was getting to be the way you would have expected her to be before. It didn't seem right.

Maybe, she thought as she started on the last nail, Miss Faine had had some terrible hold on Evelyn, the way some of the girls said. Maybe she had kept Evelyn hypnotized or something. Those awful eyes of hers could have hypnotized anybody. And Evelyn certainly acted as if she were out from under a spell, now. It would have been pretty awful to be in Miss Faine's power for years and years. Look at the way she'd treated those girls she'd caught borrowing the hospital acetone for polish remover. They kept feeling only about two jumps away from the electric chair for months.

Maybe Evelyn reached a point where she couldn't stand it and broke through the hypnotism and . . . Of course Miss Faine was supposed to have died of

214

her diabetes, but some of the girls said that tall crazy intern with good-looking eyes, the one they called Hard Boiled had thought she was murdered. Some of the girls said he'd only shut up about it because Dr. Willoughby was implicated, and he was all hero worship about Dr. Willoughby. But if Miss Faine really was murdered, Evelyn having done it made more sense. She glanced at her roommate again with faint apprehension.

You wouldn't think you could murder somebody and then come back to work a day later and begin wearing your hair looser and going out with men for the first time in your life. . . . You'd think you'd have a guilty conscience. But maybe some murderers didn't have guilty consciences. She glanced at Evelyn. She didn't look like a murderer, but better be as nice to her as you could.

"Want me to do your nails when I've finished?" she volunteered suddenly.

Evelyn didn't take her eyes from the ceiling. It was an odd offer for Kathy to make. Kathy knew she never put anything on her nails. Aunt Caroline would have been so angry. But it didn't seem any odder than anything else in this new world she had been living in since Wednesday night. "I'm too tired to move right now," she said dreamily. "I'm relieving tonight, so I think I'll just lie here and rest, but it's sweet of you, Kathy."

She wasn't really tired, but there were so many things to think about. All these things Dr. Everett had told her. They didn't seem real yet. They must be real. They had sounded real when he told them to her, but the only thing she could realize at the moment was that here she was lying the way she used to lie hating people, being afraid, and suddenly there wasn't anybody to hate, or anything to be afraid of.

Dr. Bowman knew she didn't have a father and he didn't care. Maybe other people wouldn't care either. And the funny thing about that was that now she did have a father. Dr. Everett wanted her. He had wanted her from the first moment he knew about her, and he wasn't a horrible person at all the way her mother had kept telling her. It was—it was her mother who had been the horrible person. She was able to face that fact without pain so far, because facing it made it all right to have this free floating feeling she had been having ever since her mother had—been murdered.

Murdered—and Dr. Harvey thought Dr. Everett had done it. Dr. Everett said he hadn't but he said he had wanted to, and because of her. She could see the eyes of the little man looking at her across the desk with protective warmth. He had done it because of her. The idea seemed no more fantastic than any of the other ideas she had had to accept in the past few days. And that meant he was in danger and she must

216

think of some way to help him. She couldn't let her father go to jail just as she had found him, she couldn't let him go to jail for something he had done for her.

There was a knock at the door. "Come in," chirped Kathy hopefully. Evelyn didn't move. It was never for her.

The door opened hesitatingly. A dark plump woman in an unpressed coat and frowsy hair but very direct brown eyes moved halfway through it and then stopped. "They said this was Miss Moore's room."

"Evelyn Moore?" Kathy gestured toward the bed. Evelyn sat up slowly. What would this funny-looking little woman want with her?

"I'm your Aunt Maggie Hillsley," said the woman awkwardly. "They told me last night that Caroline was dead, so I thought I'd come. I thought you might want to see some of your folks again."

"Why . . ." Evelyn was staring at her with slow difficult recognition. "Why, yes." Then her mind was suddenly cold and cautious as it jumped back nine years to that terrible Christmas Eve, the last time she had ever seen this woman. "I suppose so."

"I have to go to work now." They didn't even notice the other student as she moved tactfully out of the room. They were looking at each other, trying to bridge the nine-year gap.

217

"Won't you sit down?" said Evelyn after a long time.

"Well, if you want me to." The woman sat down heavily, and continued to stare at her niece. "Why didn't you let me know you were alone again?" she burst out suddenly. "Why didn't you come out to the farm, Evelyn? You always could have, you know."

"I didn't think about it," said Evelyn truthfully. So much had happened since that moment three days ago when Dr. Willoughby had said, "We've lost, de Grasse." She had been so busy adjusting to things, that it had never occurred to her that she was alone in the midst of trouble. Alone, why it was before that she had been alone. And if she had thought of Aunt Maggie it would never have occurred to her to go to her. The nine year old Christmas stayed vividly before her mind, the room where Aunt Caroline had taken her and told her all those horrible unforgettable things. She put her hand up to her face in the old manner at the memory of that moment, and Mrs. Hillsley must have recognized the gesture, for she said abruptly:

"It wasn't true, Evelyn, whatever she told you when she took you away, not about us anyway. We were just fond of you and wanting to have you with us. It was she who was always wanting to take people away from people. She was a hard and cruel woman, your mother, though I do say it of the dead. You'd

218

have been better off with us, and you sitting there now looking like a ghost." Her voice trembled a little with bitterness.

"I know," Evelyn whispered. "But I haven't known it very long. I haven't had time to think—what I was going to do."

"I know," echoed Mrs. Hillsley suddenly lowering her voice. "But you've got to think, don't you? She told me, that social service girl who came out last night, she told me what people were saying about you. That's why I came."

"What people are saying about me?"

"Oh, I'm not saying it's true," said Mrs. Hillsley hastily. "And if it was, nobody in the world could blame you, Caroline being what she was and having led you the life I can see she has. Nobody could blame you, that is, if the whole truth were to come out. But the truth's an ugly thing in this case, and sometimes it's better to run away from it. That's why I came," she repeated.

Evelyn was looking at her aunt blankly, struggling for coherent thought. "I don't seem to know any more what is truth," she said vaguely. "So many things have happened to break down what I thought was the truth and I haven't had time yet to sort the new facts out into any kind of order."

"And they'll never give you time once they start asking questions." The woman nodded her head.

"That girl told me what people were saying. That was why she came out, she said, to find some way of helping you, but she won't be able to help you once the police come. I know how the police are. That time our hired man was caught taking some of the next door farmer's ducks to market to sell as his own, you'd have thought they were going to hang Tom and me the questions they asked, and us knowing nothing about it. It was awful, child. I know how they'd be if they really had something to go on. You were always a timid little thing, Evelyn. You couldn't ever stand it."

"Couldn't stand it?" Evelyn almost laughed thinking how little this funny frowsy loyal aunt of hers knew about her ability to stand things. "There's nothing I haven't learned to stand, but I wouldn't have to. I didn't kill Aunt Caroline." She used the familiar name for her mother quite unconsciously, but then added quickly, thinking of the little cockatoo-tufted man with the warm brown eyes, "They aren't sure that anyone killed her, you know."

"I wasn't saying anyone did," said Mrs. Hillsley evasively, "but that girl said they were talking about it and the Lord knows you had plenty of reason to. Nobody could blame you but . . ." She broke off. "So far there's been no charges or anything, that girl said, and there's nothing to keep you here now, so what I say is you and me take Tom's insurance and take a little trip. I've been kind of pining out there on the farm since he died. I want to go where it's warm all the time. Mexico, maybe, I thought, that's out of the country. I mean," she added, "it'll be kind of foreign and interesting. We could take the money and go down there where nobody knows us and maybe even stay and grow oranges or something. It'll be real nice you and me being together again, Evelyn." Her words were awkward but her eyes were bright with anxiety.

Evelyn was oblivious to the anxiety. The thought of leaving this wonderful part of the world just as it was beginning to be so wonderful was unbearable. "Oh, no," she said. She couldn't leave Dr. Bowman— or Dr. Everett. No, she couldn't leave Dr. Everett when he was in all this trouble. She had to stay and find some way to help him get free. Help him? But Aunt Maggie thought it was she who needed help. Aunt Maggie thought it was she who had—killed Aunt Caroline. If she thought so, why, probably other people did. Other people would be sure of it if she went away. People might stop bothering Dr. Everett then. He had done it for her, and he was the head of the hospital and she was only a little student nurse. He had a lot more to lose than she had, and he had done it for her. She could leave a note saying she had done it, and once she was somewhere like Mexico they could never get at her to find out . . .

Something inside her began to go numb. It was a familiar numbness, the old feeling of resignation and hopelessness. It would be hard leaving Dr. Bowman, but some people weren't made to be happy. Everybody couldn't be. Things just happened to people. This wasn't any worse than anything else.

"When do you want to go?" she said, bringing each word out with an effort. This was the thing to do, she was telling herself. It must be, or Aunt Maggie wouldn't have happened along right now this way. This was the thing to do. It would save Dr. Everett who had done what he did to save her. It wasn't fair to have let her see how lovely life could be and then take it away, but life had never been fair. "Do you want to go soon?" she said.

"Well, I thought tomorrow," said Mrs. Hillsley almost happily. "You never know what's going to happen. I thought we'd just shut up the farm and pile the things into the truck and go. Could you get ready by tomorrow noon, child? I could meet you somewhere along the main road. Look, I'll draw you a map. You know," she said kindly, "I think we'll have a real good time, once we get away from this place where you've had so much trouble."

"You're awfully kind, Aunt Maggie," said Evelyn wearily. This place where she'd had so much trouble, yes, but the place too where she'd just begun to see

222

♥

what life could be like without trouble, and she was leaving it. But she had to do it. It was the thing to do.

"Kind?" the aunt smiled. "I think it's going to be kind of nice, you and me, and don't you worry about what I'll be thinking. I'd think a sight less of you if you'd just kept on living with her."

Evelyn didn't say anything. Later, when they were far away, she could tell Aunt Maggie that she hadn't done it, she might tell her even about Dr. Bowman, but not till they were far away, too far away to get back.

Long after her aunt had left she was still sitting on the bed holding the map, with an expression of bewildered resignation on her face. She wasn't used to happiness, she wasn't used to bending life the way she wanted it, and it was more natural, really, this yielding to fate in what seemed a good cause than any amount of fighting would have been.

She jumped when there was a knock on the door, and when a head stuck in and said, "You're wanted on the phone," she went to it almost as if in her sleep. The first pang, the first sense of what she might be losing came when a voice said, "Hello, this is Henry Bowman. Are you all right, Evelyn? Did you have a bad time?"

"Not very," she said, and was glad he'd asked that, for it brought the image of her father out clearer and stronger than the image of this tall kind spectacled person on the other end of the wire, and it needed to be clearer and stronger. "He was sweet," she added truthfully.

"When am I going to see you? His voice was impatient of this extraneous tenderness.

"I don't know." She hesitated. It would be dreadful seeing him again, telling him, and she would have to tell him—or would she? It would be more dreadful not seeing him again, and she had spent most of her life keeping things to herself. Surely she could do it a few hours longer, if it meant a few hours of that happiness she had been feeling. Then when it was over she could still have it to remember.

"I have to relieve tonight," she said, "but I'm free till eight, Henry."

XXII

SALLY pushed a lock of pale hair out of her eyes and looked accusingly at Kenny. "What a fine helpful honest woman you turned out to be," she said.

Kenny's shrug was more Kennyish than ever. "Well," she said, "it wasn't exactly my story. I couldn't see how dishing all that twenty-year-old dirt was going to help you find your old murderer—if there ever was a murderer."

"If there was a murderer. Do you think I pushed myself under that car? Because I can tell you right now, my friend, I've had experiences that were pleasanter."

"For God's sake, Kenny," Cyrus looked up over his feet which were resting on the edge of the bed supporting him precariously in a tipped-back chair.

"You aren't going to keep up this skeptic stuff, are you, not after the things I told you Everett told me only a couple of hours ago."

Kenny set her mouth grimly. "Bliss Everett is quite a man, Hard Boiled. I don't believe he murdered Caroline Faine. I don't believe there was that much violence in him. But if he did, he had plenty of provocation and you haven't got any sort of case against him. You haven't got one single fact that would stand up."

Cyrus sighed. "I know it," he said.

"So what then. Drop it. Everett's a swell guy. Faine, for all she was a friend of mine, had a pretty bitchy streak in her. So drop it. It's just going to mean more people getting hurt, if you don't."

Cyrus sighed again. "I know it," he repeated. "But Willoughby's a swell guy too. I'm a swell guy in my own rather peculiar way. What about our reputations, old girl? What about that Chair of Medicine? If this thing isn't broken by Monday there's no Chair of Medicine for Willoughby, so if I'm going to do it, and I am going to do it, I've got to work fast."

"I'll say you have." Kenny's voice was derisive. "Any plans?"

Cyrus shrugged Kennyishly. "I've an idea," he said. "I think maybe I'll get a confession."

Kenny gave a short laugh. "You think Everett,

supposing Caroline Faine was murdered and supposing Everett did it, is going to tell you all about it and then sign on the dotted line? Confidence is a beautiful thing, Hard Boiled."

"Well," said Cyrus slowly as if thinking aloud, "he almost did this afternoon. He told me plenty. I almost wish he hadn't, about that liquor prescription stuff for instance, but he did and I'm going to use it. He thinks I'm going to the police. Well, I'm not, yet. I'm going back to him tomorrow and tell him if he'll confess, using Faine's threats as a motive, I'll keep Evelyn out of it. I think that'll work. I'm almost sure it will. He must be pretty sick of the whole business by now."

Kenny looked at him curiously. "Want to make a small bet on it?" she asked softly.

Cyrus got up and shook his mussed white ducks. "Sure," he said. "Fix up the details with my secretary here." He blew out his breath. "This afternoon having been pure recreation I now have to go to work, and I mean work. Ever see a real case of aspirin allergy, Kenny?"

She shook her head. "I've read about them. Is he bad?"

"Well, he may live, but his larynx is swelled up so he can't any more than just breathe, even with adrenalin. Probably a tracheotomy is on the books before the night's over, which will be fun. And maybe even that won't save him."

"Kind of rare, isn't it?" Kenny showed professional interest.

"The books say so. Never seems rare to me because I've got the same trouble, believe it or not. Found it out when I was about thirteen and had tonsillitis. Nearly died myself. Since then I've kept away from aspirin."

Sally looked up wonderingly from her bed. "You haven't got six toes or anything?" she asked. "The things I find out about you every day. What else are you allergic to?"

He grinned absentmindedly. "You'll find out in time. Nothing that cramps my style noticeably. Aspirin doesn't. I don't get headaches often enough."

"If you did, you ought to have a honey of a one right now," Kenny remarked caustically.

Cyrus was still grinning. "Matter of fact, I have," he said. "A hell of a one, and I'll bet I have a worse one before I break this thing."

Kenny looked at him steadily and there was an odd light in her eye. "You aren't going to break it, brother," she said. "But I'll say this much for you, I think if anyone could you'd be the one. That fantastic stuff inside your skull that people call brain." She shook her head. "I'd hate to be in the way when you get going."

228

Cyrus looked down at the monkeyish little figure in white. "I'd hate to have you, old girl."

The aspirin patient wasn't doing so well when he got over on the ward. It looked as if that tracheotomy was pretty imminent. He started to call surgery and then realized that Willoughby hadn't seen the patient. Be only manners to call him, and he might have an idea, though it would be hard to know what. They had already tried about everything. Well, call him anyway. The operator got him at the third hospital she tried, which was pretty fair.

"Dr. Willoughby?"

"Hello, Harvey."

"We've got a patient here, sir, pretty bad." Cyrus told him the details.

Willoughby didn't have anything new to suggest but to call a surgical consultant. He sounded in a hurry. But Cyrus wouldn't let him go quite yet.

"About that bottle, sir?"

"Oh, that bottle, Harvey. I've been meaning to call you all day, but I've been rushed off my feet, haven't even had any lunch." Willoughby's voice was apologetic. "It's very peculiar about that bottle, Harvey. I put it in my overcoat pocket. You saw me, you know, but when I got home it was gone."

Cyrus had a feeling almost of nausea inside him. His only link with fact. Not, as everyone pointed out, that it was much, but it was something. And he'd had a hunch he ought to hold onto it. "Did you leave your coat anywhere, sir?" he asked as calmly as he could.

"I don't think so. Yes, I did. I stopped by to speak to Dr. Everett about Miss Pepper, left my coat in the hall of the Administration Building. You see—anyone could have got at it."

"Did you mention it to Dr. Everett?"

"No, Harvey, I thought . . ."

"I understand," said Cyrus hurriedly.

"I can't tell you how much I regret this." The chief sounded genuinely disturbed. "But perhaps we can think of something else. I won't be able to get out until tomorrow morning. I realize how important this is to us both, but one's patients, unfortunately, have to come first."

"Of course, sir, don't give it a thought," Cyrus spoke politely. "I don't really know," he added, "that it makes much difference." And it really didn't, he told himself, trying to banish that sinking feeling. If what he had in mind, if what he was setting in progress worked out, a little thing like a bottle of phony insulin with a number on it was going to look pretty insignificant.

XXIII

SUNDAY morning, and Cyrus was walking draggingly along the long corridor toward his ward. Sunday morning. Sunday was supposed to be the day of rest, just as Saturday night was supposed to be the night to go places. Go places and do things. Well, what he'd done was work all night on that aspirin allergy, that and think about what he was going to have to do today to trap a murderer. Trapping sounded fine and romantic and frontier-like, but it didn't make romantic thinking. It was going to be a hell of a mess, and Cyrus knew it. It was going to cause a hell of a lot of trouble for a lot of basically swell people. It hardly seemed worth it. Yet, if you didn't, well, there was Willoughby; there was himself and that zoo full

231

of grinning, sneering interns; there was little Sally being pushed under that car. All night his mind had kept shying away from the conflict, and to bring it back he had brought up the picture of Sally falling under the wheels of the car he was driving. Then he had been able to think about it some more, and he had to think, think plenty. You couldn't go through with a thing like this unless you knew exactly what you were going to do if other people turned out to do certain other things you had a hunch they might. He shook his head to clear it. God, he felt lousy. If only he could put the whole thing off, an hour, half an hour, fifteen minutes.

He was passing the Children's Ward. If Kenny was in there he could stop and say hello and . . . He hesitated, glanced at his watch, hesitated a moment more, then turned quickly into the wing.

"Miss Kenny around?"

"In her office," the nurse at the desk indicated the frosted glass door. He tapped on it and stuck his head in.

"Hello, Kenny. Thought you'd like to know I haven't got that confession yet, but I'm on my way."

"Bad luck to you." She closed the drawer of her desk and leaned back. Her smile was tired. This thing is getting her too, he thought. "What's the Pepper kid doing up and around?" she went on. "She's out there in the ward this minute chumming around with the kids as if it were six months since she'd seen them instead of two days. If you ask me she looks like hell. Who let her out?"

"Don't you know by this time? Nobody lets Sally do anything. She lets herself and goes ahead."

"It must be great to love children that much."

"Why, Kenny, don't you love children?"

"Not many people I love." She shrugged. "Hate's more in my line." She got up. "Better tell Pepper you're here or she'll chew my ear off."

"Wait a minute." He flopped into a chair as if exhausted. "Between you and me, Kenny, I feel like hell myself. I'm on my way to do something damn unpleasant and get some perfectly nice people into a lot of trouble." His face was white.

"Everett?"

"Among others. I've got one little thing to attend to, then I'm going to the police and tell what I know."

"Think what you know is enough?"

"Enough to give me a perfectly swell headache just thinking about it. And only last night I was saying I never missed aspirin. Right now my head feels like it was going to open right up and invite inspection."

"Take something else, dope."

"Maybe I will. Got any pyramidon?"

"Sure you're not allergic to that? People are. What happened to the other guy who couldn't take aspirin?"

"He's dead. Tracheotomy wasn't enough, Kenny.
It was a lousy death."

She stared. "The things you run across in a city
hospital. Well, we wouldn't like to lose that great
mind of yours that way. Pyramidon?"

"Make it about three. Nothing less would touch
me." He sat slumped into his seat relaxing, making
his mind as blank as possible for the few brief minutes he still could. Maybe by tonight he could go
back to just being an intern. When was it he used
to gripe at the regimented life interns led? No chance
for responsibility, no chance for initiative?—hell,
right now it sounded like heaven. He put his head in
his hands and tried not to think until Kenny came
back with a small medicine glass containing some
white tablets in one hand and a glass of water in the
other.

"Here," she said with what for Kenny amounted to
solicitude. "This'll fix you up. I couldn't find the
Pepper kid. Maybe she had a brainstorm and went
back to bed like a normal human being."

"You wouldn't be speaking about me?" Sally's fair
head stuck itself in the door as Cyrus took the glass
and swallowed down the pills. "Matter, Cy? Never
saw you take medicine before."

"Never saw me need it before." He looked at her
critically. Her face was very pale, her gray eyes were
hollow and she spoke with an effort. "Looks to me

like you need something or other yourself. Little rest in bed, maybe."

"I'm going back pretty soon." She came into the little room. There was a letter in one hand and she was tapping it restlessly against the other palm. "It's awfully dull up there and I got to wondering how the kids were. Glad I did too. Somebody has been writing me fan letters. Found this in my desk. Maybe it'll give me something to dream about when I get back to bed." Her words were casual, but her eyes on his face were anxious. "You do look like the devil, Cy. What's the matter?"

"Just that headache you and Kenny were wishing on me last night. It'll be gone in a few minutes now."

"It ought to be. The guy took three pyramidons." Kenny was wandering restlessly around the little room.

"Pyramidon? Of course. He couldn't take aspirin, could he?" Sally's eyes were still anxiously on Cyrus' face.

"Not much difference unless you're . . ." Cyrus coughed and put his hand up to his throat. "One of those pills must have stuck on the way down. Give me the rest of that water, will you? Thanks." He coughed again and tried to draw a deep breath, but all that came was a short hard gasp.

"Cy," said Sally sharply, "what's the matter?" Kenny was watching him now too.

He tried to speak but couldn't, only shook his head, and his hands were clenched so tight that the knuckles stood out.

"Kenny," said Sally, "do something, for heaven's sake! He's choking to death. What did you give him?"

"What he asked for, pyramidon. Maybe he's allergic to that too, and didn't know it." The usually efficient nurse stood there looking at Cyrus with uncertainty and fright in her eyes.

"Well, do something!" There was terror in Sally's voice.

"I'll get a hypodermic of adrenalin. That ought to fix him up. If it doesn't right away we'll call Medical and . . ." Kenny disappeared out the door leaving the sentence trailing.

Sally stood gripping Cyrus' hand as the gasping grew worse. She reached down and loosened his collar and tie. Her forehead was dripping with sweat and her hands were trembling. His eyes tried to reassure her but the harsh rasping of his breath didn't stop.

"Here," Kenny was back, a glass of water in one hand and a syringe in the other. "Roll up his sleeve now, Pepper, and we'll fix him up." Her voice was rough with emotion.

Her hand holding the hypodermic reached toward Cyrus. He straightened up and grasped it with his own, his breath suddenly coming perfectly normally, if a little fast. "I don't think so, Kenny. Close the door, Sal, we've got some things to talk about, we three."

"What is this?" Kenny spoke angrily. "One of your lousy jokes?"

Cyrus stood there, still holding her hand, looking down at it. "Lord, Kenny, I wish it were. Let's have that hypodermic, old girl. I'm sort of anxious to find out what's in it. We've had a lot of trouble having things analyzed around here recently, but maybe we can manage to hold onto this, and"—his other hand opened and showed a partly crushed tablet—"this too. What bottle'd you see her get it out of, Sally?"

"The aspirin bottle," Sally almost whispered the words. "Oh, Kenny, how could you?"

"How could I what?" Kenny's voice was rough. "Maybe I made a mistake, but I thought I was giving him pyramidon."

Sally shook her head and there were sudden tears in her eyes. "I was standing behind the door watching you. You looked at the label a long time as if you were trying to decide something. You didn't make a mistake, Kenny."

"What were you doing behind the door, Pepper? That's going to be kind of hard to explain."

"No, it's not," said Cyrus quietly. "She was waiting to see if you were going to try choking me off with

237

aspirin. You must have been pretty anxious to shut me up, Kenny. to try that after I told you the other man died."

"You must be crazy, Harvey." Kenny tried to laugh. "All this detecting has addled your brain. This is just about in a piece with all your other bright ideas. I make a mistake, that's all. I'm darn sorry, but anybody can make a mistake." She tried to laugh again. "Nurses are famous for it."

Cyrus shook his head. "You didn't make a mistake, Kenny. We're the ones that have been making the mistakes, until last night. I always thought there was something funny about your friendship with Caroline Faine. It never did make sense, but I figured you were both queer ducks of different sorts and that was all. Until last night. Last night, Kenny, when you were talking about Bliss Everett there was something in your voice and face that had never been there before. And you forgot for a moment that Caroline Faine was supposed to be a good friend of yours. It gave me a wild hunch, but one that fitted in with all the other things I knew. I thought I'd give you a chance to prove it for me, Kenny." He lifted his shoulders. "You proved it all right. I wish like hell you hadn't."

Kenny still shook her head as if in bewilderment. "I'm lost," she said. "What've I proved?"

"That Bliss Everett was important enough to you,"

238

said Cyrus slowly, "for you not only to get rid of Caroline Faine, whom you hated, to save his reputation, but also to try to get rid of both Sally and me, whom you used to kind of like. Maybe you can't understand it, Kenny old girl, but I've a hunch the police will."

Sally was looking at Kenny. Tears were rolling down her cheeks now. "Oh, Kenny, how could you?" she whispered again. "We loved you, Kenny."

"Love." The nurse laughed a hard little laugh. "Try having someone you're crazy about kiss you just once, then never look at you again except with respect for twenty years. Try watching him worship for most of that time at the lousy altar of a female sadist who thought it was fun to take him away from you, a female sadist who thought it would be still more fun to break him when the moment suited her. Try that if you want to know something about love."

"I figured it like that," said Cyrus quietly. "I knew if you killed her you had a damn good reason, Kenny."

"You bet I had a good reason, so good I didn't care what happened to me if it got her too. I'd watched that bitch playing with Bliss Everett's heart for twenty years. I wasn't going to stand by and see her take away the only thing he had left. I knew all about it, you see. I was her friend—she thought." She gave another little laugh that was like breaking glass.

239

"Lord, I had trouble not to laugh when I took that vase of forget-me-nots to her just before she died and she looked so pleased. She didn't know it was my little joke for a change, my tribute to her confidences. She used to get a lot of pleasure out of telling me about Everett. She wasn't dumb, except about my friendship. She guessed how I was about Everett. That was half the fun of telling me. That was more than half my fun when I realized I could stop her for good by taking something away from her for a change, something she needed."

"And it looked so easy, didn't it, Kenny, so foolproof." Cyrus' voice was almost a whisper. "It almost was, wasn't it?"

"I wouldn't have tried it if it hadn't been. I was doing it to keep the guy out of trouble, not involve him." She looked down for a minute and her face contracted painfully. "Well, I've certainly botched things—with your help. Why couldn't you leave the thing alone? I warned you. I tried to tell you you were getting in over your depth. I tried to get at those records that gave you a lead before you did, and when I couldn't I tried to scare you away. I wasn't going to kill you then, Harvey, just show you this wasn't anything to fool with. But you wouldn't scare, you were too bright and brave for that—and too dumb. Hell, why don't they teach kids about life these days, instead of letting them run around loose in diapers? Maybe if they knew something about emotion they'd have more respect for it."

"Even if we'd suspected, even if we'd known, what else could we have done?" said Sally hopelessly.

"Shut your eyes. You wouldn't be the first. It was justice I was doing." The words were grim.

"Justice, sure, but it turned out to be injustice too, Kenny," Cyrus reminded her. "They don't seem to go separately. One injustice started you. Another injustice started me. Maybe we should have both put our hands behind our backs, but we couldn't seem to."

"What injustice started you?" There was the breaking glass again. "You mean your dear chief Lester Willoughby. Let me go for a minute." She pulled at her hand which was still in his grasp. "I won't try to get away. Where would I go and what would it get me? Matter of fact, it's kind of restful knowing it's all over and no more thinking to be done. Let me go, Cy, for a second. I want to show you something kind of interesting I'd just found when you came in."

He didn't let her go, though something inside of him turned over at hearing her say Cy when she never had before, hearing her say it unconsciously, now that they were not nurse and intern but two people with neither defense nor pretense. She was a swell old gal and she liked him. It didn't matter that she had just tried to kill him. But he didn't let go of her arm. He walked with her behind the desk and carefully watched her open the top drawer and take something out with her free hand. He only let her go when she held it toward him. "Ever see this before?"

He took it and turned it over slowly and his eyes widened. It was a bottle of crystalline insulin and the control number was 94459.

"So you took it out of his pocket again," he said. "I thought you must have. But why show it to me? Why haven't you destroyed it?"

"I should take it out of his pocket," Kenny sounded almost jaunty for a moment, "after getting such pleasure out of putting it into his bag. Sure I put it there. I got it out of the lab icebox early that morning. I knew you were going to have it analyzed and there weren't many other places you could have left it. After breakfast I was passing the parking lot and there was his car, and bang, the idea came to me. I never did like the man after the soft way he helped Caroline cover up for herself. Kind of funny, I thought"—she was actually grinning for a moment—"making him help cover up her murder. Don't look so worried, Pepper, no sense lying about it now. If I do, this guy might try to pin the thing on Everett. If I don't, well, maybe we can still keep him out of it somehow.

"Sure I put it in Willoughby's bag, but why should

242

I take it out of his pocket, why should I know it was there even? Nope, Cy, that bottle just appeared here in my desk drawer, and the reason I haven't destroyed it is I just found it. I didn't open the drawer yesterday, too busy, but I opened it just now and there it was. Do you make of it what I do?"

"I don't make anything of it." Cyrus' voice was stubborn.

"Well, try," she taunted him. "Start with that swell chief of yours who was too good a diabetic specialist not to figure out what was wrong with Caroline Faine. That had you worried, didn't it, and why? Because you were darn right he was too good. Because sure he figured it out, or half figured it, anyway." She looked up, her monkeyish face wrinkled maliciously.

"Remember that afternoon I relieved Evelyn, the afternoon after Caroline came into the Infirmary and Willoughby had changed the brand? You told me that yourself, Cy. Quite a help you were, right along. Well, I knew what brand he switched to, dropped over at lunchtime to commiserate with my dear friend, and found that out, so I had the right kind of bottle snug in my pocket. They aren't very big, they don't make much of a bulge. And," she snorted, "I changed it right then and there while you were all gathered worshipfully around the bed, while I was straightening things so there'd be no mess to annoy the sick directress. Only Willoughby saw me do it that time. He doesn't miss much, I'll say that for him. He turned around just as I was at the medicine tray and saw me put something in my pocket. I think he'd been looking for something like that to account for the lady's ailments. He had to know, but that was enough, that satisfied his diagnostic brain. Doing something would have caused a scandal and stirred up that other old scandal. Willoughby didn't want any scandals, not that would involve him, however remotely, especially not right now. It never occurred to him, probably, that he'd have this other negligence scandal to live down. He was too sure of his reputation for that, a lot surer, as it turns out, than he had any right to be." Cyrus started to interrupt, but Kenny wouldn't let him. Her voice went on.

"Kind of a relief too probably, to have the old bitch out of the way. Nobody could play nursemaid to Caroline Faine for twenty years without thinking how swell it would be to see her dead, particularly a guy like Willoughby who'd got nothing but kicks in return for all his nursing. So just let it slide, just relax and give your mind a rest, that was the easiest way, and the safest."

"You don't know this," said Cyrus. "You're just guessing, just trying to drag someone else in."

"How else would I have got the bottle? I thought it was still in his bag. It must have made him see red to find that bottle wished on him, made him see such

244

red all he could think of was getting back at me, reminding me, not too pleasantly, that I wasn't getting away with anything either. Perfectly safe, too, unless I was discovered, and how could anyone discover me? That's where he slipped up." She gave a hard harsh crackle.

"I don't believe it," said Cyrus again but with less conviction.

"I do," said Sally suddenly. "It fits too well not to be true."

"Sure it does." Kenny sat suddenly down by the desk as if she couldn't stand any longer. "Well, what happens next?" she asked with flippant indifference that fooled neither Cyrus nor Sally.

Cyrus didn't answer right away. He stood by her, turning the little bottle over and over. "Your telephone number's been behind all this, Sal," he said. "I'm not going to like calling it much from now on." He glanced sideways at Kenny. She was fumbling in the back of the drawer. He started to reach for her arm to check it, but glanced at her face again and then glanced away.

"Look, Sally," he said quickly, "suppose you run across the hall to the other office and call Everett. Try to get Willoughby too. I think he's in the ward. I was on my way over to meet him there. Ask them both to come down here, will you? I think," his voice was a little thin, "when you tell them I'm asking and that it's important they'll come. Thanks, kid." He was shoving her toward the door. "We'll wait for them here."

When he turned back to the desk Kenny was just putting down the glass of water that she had brought for him. She was smiling almost impishly. "Thanks, Cy," she said. "It's probably as close as you'll ever come, being you, to breaking your Hippocratic oath, but I won't be around to tell." Her breath was coming in shorter and shorter gasps as she finished. She opened her mouth and a low strangled cry came out, then her eyes lost all recognition.

Cyrus stood perfectly still a yard from the desk, watching her. It wasn't fun to watch. Probably cyanide, a part of his mind registered, nothing else would work so fast, probably potassium cyanide that she had hidden away back there for just this emergency, but the rest of him was racked with pity and horror at the unbelievable violence accompanying sudden death. There was nothing he could do, nothing he wanted to do, but the horror was there.

When her body was finally still, slumped down behind the desk, he went around and with his stethoscope automatically listened for the heart which he knew must have stopped beating. Then he straightened up and went slowly to the door.

Sally was coming out of the other office with terror in her eyes as he locked it on the other side. "Where is she?" she whispered. "What happened? I thought I heard her cry. What did she . . ."

Cyrus raised his shoulders in a gesture that was more a memorial to Kenny than anything he could have said. "You wouldn't have wanted me to stop her."

XXIV

THEY stood there by the door avoiding each other's eyes until Dr. Everett arrived. They could hear the murmur of voices in the ward just beyond, the bustle of nurses tending to their usual routine, unconscious of that short, sharp, strangled cry. Hospitals, after all, are accustomed to violence and death, too accustomed to be extraordinarily sensitive, and most children, even most ward children in a big city hospital, are oblivious to it.

Dr. Everett when he turned the corner of the wing and hastened toward them seemed less so. There was alarm in his step and in the very jut of his cockatoo tuft of gray hair. But his voice when he spoke was as calm and controlled as ever. "What is it, Harvey? I gather from Miss Pepper it must be fairly urgent."

248

Cyrus didn't speak. He found all at once that he couldn't. Sally didn't speak either as he unlocked the door of the office and waited for the superintendent to precede him.

"Is something the matter with Miss Kenny?" Everett asked. "Where is she, Harvey?"

Cyrus still couldn't speak. There hadn't been any lump in his throat earlier, but there was now. He gestured toward the desk. He moved around behind it and guided Dr. Everett with his eyes.

Sally stood forlorn and forgotten by the door as Dr. Everett moved to follow Cyrus' eyes, then looked up to meet them, his own widening with horror. He stooped over behind the desk for what seemed to Sally forever, then slowly straightened up. "What happened?" he said. "Did you find her this way, Harvey?"

"No, sir," Cyrus managed to get out the words. "I was right here when she did it. You see . . ."

There was a knock at the door. The smooth face of Dr. Willoughby appeared as Sally opened it.

"What is it, Miss Pepper? What's happened? Oh, hello, Bliss, glad to see you here too. Good morning, Harvey. Is anything wrong?"

Cyrus looked at Everett, waiting for him to speak. He didn't for a minute.

"I'm afraid so, Lester," he said at last. "I'm afraid we have a very terrible tragedy on our hands. Miss

Kenny . . ." He motioned to the other doctor to come and look.

Willoughby kneeled over the body. "It must have just happened," he said after a moment. "What caused it? Was anybody here?" His face had a stiff masklike look as if he were trying to conceal emotion.

"Harvey was just telling me," said Everett and there was a grim note in his voice. "He says he was here when it happened. Go on, Harvey."

"It must have been cyanide," said Cyrus slowly. "It happened so quickly. She was unconscious in not much more than a minute, I think." He reached over and rummaged around in the desk and gingerly brought out a folded paper cup and still more gingerly held it not too near his nose. "She must have had it in here."

"You tried to stop her, of course."

"No, sir." Cyrus looked the little superintendent in the eye. "You see, she had just confessed to the murder of Miss Faine."

"Confessed—to murder. But this is fantastic, Harvey. Why would she? Whatever would have prompted her?"

"Because," said Cyrus slowly, "I had just caught her in an attempt to murder me."

"Harvey, you must be losing your mind," Everett spoke sharply.

"I'd probably agree with you, sir," Cyrus tried to

smile but it wouldn't come, "but Miss Pepper was right here with me. She saw it happen."

Everett turned questioningly to Sally. She found she was shaking as she tried to speak. "Yes," she said incoherently. "I saw her get down the bottle of aspirin and look at it carefully before she shook out the tablets. She knew what she was doing. There was a dreadful detached look in her eyes. I was hiding behind the door and I saw her. Then when I saw Cy begin to choke and gasp I was so frightened. I thought perhaps he had been telling the truth after all. I thought perhaps she had given him something still more dangerous."

Cyrus did smile now, a tired smile. "Let me tell them, Sal," he said. "From the beginning, hm?" He faced the other two men.

"You see," he said, "all along, even when it looked as if everything pointed to either one or the other of you, I kept feeling that whoever murdered Miss Faine almost had to be a nurse. On purely practical grounds a man would have had a hell of a time getting into the nurses' home to change those first bottles of insulin before Miss Faine was brought to the Infirmary. Dr. Willoughby might have, of course, because he was seeing Miss Faine in her room there, but other things seemed to rule out Dr. Willoughby." He didn't look at his chief as he spoke. "And then there was the psychological angle. I couldn't see a skilled, highly trained doctor murdering anyone the way Miss Faine was murdered. The way I figured it, no one who had had years of training saving lives, could bear to stand around and see someone die for the want of something they were perfectly able to supply. A good doctor might kill by a knife or a gun or poison, but not by the withdrawal of a drug. At least that was the way I figured it." He did glance at Willoughby now but only for a moment. The chief had a benign approving look on his face that made him turn quickly back to Everett.

"Even yesterday, sir," he said, "even when it looked as if you were just about admitting the murder, I still didn't believe it. I still thought it had to be a woman, and the way Evelyn Moore acted then made me sure that it wasn't she, even if I hadn't already been sure by the fact that she was out of the hospital when Sally was shoved in front of that car. I suddenly realized that about the only other person connected with Miss Faine's past was Miss Kenny. It was a long hunch, but I figured that if she had already tried to get rid of Sally, she wouldn't balk much at trying to get rid of me if I gave her a good chance. So I did."

"Weren't you taking rather a risk, Harvey?" murmured Dr. Willoughby. Cyrus glanced up and glanced away again.

"Not really, sir. Miss Kenny wouldn't have tried

anything that couldn't be covered up, because her chief motive in the whole thing was to stop any scandal that might hurt Dr. Everett's reputation, that and of course a twenty-year-old jealousy and hate. So I cooked up a story about being allergic to aspirin, dangerously allergic—that man over on the ward gave me the idea—and she fell for it. I came in asking for pyramidon and of course she gave me aspirin. Sally was watching from behind the drug-room door. She didn't want to. She didn't believe it could be true, but I persuaded her." He stopped and shut his eyes a second, then opened them as if with an effort.

"I took two of the tablets—thought I'd better save one for evidence if I needed it—and pretended to get edema of the larynx. It couldn't have been a very convincing act, but Miss Kenny'd probably never seen edema of the larynx. It's not that common. She was expecting it and pretty nervous, I guess, too nervous to be critical.

"I don't think she wanted to kill me, but she figured she had to and she was going to. Of course it wasn't a sure way of getting rid of me, but she probably thought that if nothing else I'd be too busy having a tracheotomy to cause any more trouble. Besides," he picked the hypodermic up off the desk, "when Sally insisted she do something she ran to get me this. I didn't take it. I put it up to her right then and after awhile she broke down. I think she was glad to. But my guess is that it contains the one to one hundred adrenalin instead of the ordinary kind. At least that's what I'd have done." He gave a faint weary grin.

"Kenny's and my minds worked pretty much the same way always. That's why we got along. That's probably why I was able to figure what she might do. We'll have to see about the hypo, though I don't know as it makes much difference now, but if it is the extra strong kind it would have polished me off, and could only at the very worst have been called criminal negligence. It still wouldn't have involved anyone else." He looked directly at Everett, then as he still said nothing turned and looked at Willoughby.

"A very brilliant piece of work, Harvey," murmured the chief. "My congratulations. It's most regrettable, the whole thing, but I should say you have handled it remarkably well."

Everett didn't say anything for a long moment. There was misery in his face. "A little scandal, a little damaged reputation," he said heavily at last, "would have been a small price to pay to avoid any part of this, and the tragedy is," he lifted his shoulders wearily, "it hasn't even served the purpose it all happened for. Everything will have to be told, of course." He looked at Willoughby and his face lightened a little. "Everything of course must be told," he said more firmly, "and I can't tell you, Les, how glad that

254

makes me for you. If nothing else, the airing of this whole miserable affair will completely kill all this fantastic talk that has been going around about your handling of Miss Faine's case. I myself will go to one of the trustees today. I think," he nodded thoughtfully, "that will be the best thing. I want you to have that Chair, Les; you deserve it. You'll fill it adequately." He turned to Cyrus and smiled faintly. "The hospital owes you something of an apology, Harvey, too," he said. "May I make it now officially. I imagine the interns will make it in some other more colorful way when they know. I suppose," the faint smile faded as he reached for the phone, "the thing to do now is call the police."

"Just a second, Dr. Everett," said Cyrus. "There's one other thing. This." He turned to Dr. Willoughby and held out a small bottle. "Miss Kenny said she found this in her desk this morning. I thought naturally she had stolen it from you, but she said not, and I don't think she was lying. She—but perhaps you know what she said." His words were matter of fact, but his eyes were pleading.

Dr. Willoughby took the bottle almost gingerly and looked at it expressionlessly. "No," he said then, still expressionlessly, "she might have said a good many things at that point, Harvey. Which ones did she choose?"

"She said the person who put that bottle in her

255

desk must obviously have known that she murdered Miss Faine." Cyrus hesitated. "She said it was you, sir," he finished in a burst.

"Did she say why I would have been apt to?"

"Yes," Cyrus dragged the word out miserably and unwillingly. "She said you were obviously too good a doctor not to have suspected something phony about the way Miss Faine's diabetes was acting. She knew she was taking that chance, but she didn't care by then. She says she knew you were looking for something wrong somewhere, and that you saw her switch the bottles once, but kept silent to avoid a scandal. She said you must have seen red when she tried to get rid of the bottle by dropping it in your bag, and threw it back at her to show her she wasn't getting away with anything. I didn't believe it, sir," he finished almost angrily, "but that's what she said, and there's the bottle"—his eyes fell to his chief's hand—"and I never understood how I managed to figure something out that you couldn't."

Dr. Willoughby looked at the bottle and turned it over once or twice. He glanced at Everett who was standing motionlessly intent, then he glanced at Cyrus and down at the bottle again. There was an almost unbearable sadness on his face. "It's a funny thing," he said at last, "how true a thing can be and still be the most colossal lie in the world. It frightens me, oh, not for myself, but for everybody, because

256

then what is innocence and what is guilt? Miss Kenny was guilty of murder. We all think she did a fine thing, and yet she was guilty, so guilty there was nothing to do but take her own life. And if she is guilty, perhaps I, who am innocent, am guilty too."

Sally huddled unnoticed in her corner. There was no place for feminine softness in this moment, perhaps no place for softness of any kind. Dr. Everett moved as if in protest and then was silent. Cyrus' face was stiff and his eyes were not happy.

"I did see Miss Kenny put something in her pocket, you see, the afternoon after we changed the insulin," went on Dr. Willoughby. "She's quite right about that. But I didn't know what I had seen until it was too late. Probably I should have. I was looking for something to account for Miss Faine's sudden illness. I thought I had thought of everything. I imagine I actually had thought of everything but that. The question is," his words came slowly and critically, "why didn't I think of that when it was staring me right in the face? Was it simple inability to think in terms of murder or was it," he paused, "subconscious desire to see Miss Kenny get away with what she was doing? Frankly I don't like to ask myself."

"But that's crazy, sir," Cyrus protested, "why would you have wanted her to get away with it?"

Willoughby smiled, but there was no humor in the smile. "As a doctor I wouldn't have, of course. As a doctor I was fighting to save the life of Caroline Faine. As a doctor I was trying with every conscious brain cell to think what force was behind her illness and outwit it. But nobody's all doctor, Harvey." He paused and turned slightly toward Everett. "I'd been infatuated with Caroline Faine along with you and all the other young medical fools. That was why I was willing to help her when she came to me needing help. I did help her, though in the process very completely losing my infatuation." There was momentary bitter humor in his face. "Caroline was impressive during that crisis, but rather the way a steam roller is impressive. She was hardly lovable, particularly as I gradually discovered the facts about you, Bliss, about Miss Kenny, about de Grasse. She didn't mean to tell me so much, but she felt very sure of my loyalty, with reason, I like to think. It was highly instructive to a young man training himself to observe human behavior. She lost me as a suitor, but she kept me as a doctor. Twenty years now, twenty years I've watched what she was doing to both of you. It wasn't fun to watch, particularly as I knew quite well what she could do to people." His jaw contracted for a moment, then relaxed and he looked at Everett almost mildly. "It seems quite possible to me that the part of me that wasn't clinical, bitterly wanted Caroline to suffer for what she had done—to all of us. I don't know, but this much is true. The minute

258

Harvey told me about the ineffective dose of insulin he had taken, I knew exactly what had happened and how it had happened and who had done it, and I had a sudden uncomfortable conviction that I ought to have known it all along."

"But Dr. Willoughby," Cyrus' mind was back outside the autopsy room when he had first brought the subject up. He could see again the sagging of his chief's face, the haggard stricken look, but he didn't want to see it. "But sir," he protested, "when I told you, I could have sworn you didn't believe me."

"I didn't want to believe you. I wanted Miss Kenny to go free. I felt that justice was all on her side and then there was the scandal—to the hospital, to all of us. It was too late to do anything about it then. It seemed better just to shut my mind. But when Miss Kenny tried to implicate me I felt she had to know she couldn't push me too far. I didn't want actually to accuse her. I couldn't face that, but I hoped that letting her know I knew might make her go away, somewhere far away from all of us. That was why I put the bottle in her drawer, Harvey." He turned to Cyrus now and smiled again without humor. "It's not a very satisfactory explanation, but it's the best I have to offer."

"You're being morbid, Les," Dr. Everett was soothing. "Perhaps you did see something you only understood later on, but we've all done that, often.

You're just torturing yourself unnecessarily, you know. Now I'm going to call the police and tell them what has happened. I doubt if they'd take these self-accusations very seriously, and as a friend I hope you won't feel you must air them." He reached for the phone.

"Bringing the police in isn't going to help the hospital," Willoughby said slowly, "or you, Bliss, or—your daughter."

"I know," Everett's voice was steady, "but we've a violent death on our hands and truth is truth."

"Is it?" said Willoughby. "I wonder." He looked at Cyrus. "What do you think we ought to do, Harvey? After all, this is your case."

Cyrus looked away. "I don't know. I don't know what else there is to do."

"Don't you?" Willoughby probed. "I had an idea you would, Harvey."

Cyrus looked back at him. Their eyes met for a long steady moment, then Cyrus' widened and shifted away. He shook his head slightly, then looked back at Dr. Willoughby who was still looking at him, then he reached for the phone. "Let me make that call, Dr. Everett," he said and picked it up.

"Operator, give me the City Coroner's office. Coroner's office? Is Dr. Bulmer there? Hello, Dr. Bulmer? This is Harvey at the City Hospital. Got something for your office out here. Yeah . . . A suicide . . . Yeah, a perfectly clear-cut case. Cyanide poisoning, I think . . . I found it . . . In the nurses' office on the Kid Ward. Yeah, lovely for the kiddies. . . . No, but the woman had been under a strain. Her best friend died a few days ago and she was always a queer duck. . . . No, not too surprising. . . . Sure, sure I'll wait right here till you get out." His eyes had been on his chief's face all the time he was speaking. The words were Cyrus', but the impression he gave was somehow of a person repeating dictation.

When he put down the receiver he raised one eyebrow questioningly, and Dr. Willoughby nodded slightly. There was a silence, then Willoughby said drily, "It's not really surprising, I suppose, that Miss Kenny should have committed suicide out of grief for her friend. They were very devoted. Perhaps she could have taken it better, if she hadn't felt all along that the case had somehow been mismanaged. It was impossible, apparently, to make her understand that insulin fastness does occur. Rather grim, for you, Harvey, discovering it this way."

"Yes, sir," Cyrus' face was as expressionless as one with his vitality could be. "Particularly after all the crazy things I'd cooked up in my mind about the whole business. But the hell with that."

Dr. Everett was shaking his head. "You can't do it, Harvey, or you either, Les. I won't let you. I can't tell you how grateful I am for myself and Evelyn and for the hospital, but the thing has got to come out."

"What thing?" asked Cyrus. "You must have had other interns go temporarily bats, Dr. Everett, when they've had too heavy a schedule. Maybe not to the point of imagining murders and attempted murders around every corner, but that's a matter of degree. The whole thing must have been in my mind, because, as you have both pointed out, there isn't a shred of evidence to the contrary."

Dr. Willoughby moved his hand slightly. Cyrus glanced down and saw the little bottle in it. He reached out and took it and began to work casually at the cap. "Well, I've snapped out of it and snapped out of it good," he said. "Good thing I couldn't convince the rest of you to make jackasses out of yourselves." He wandered over to the washstand in the corner and turned on the hot water.

Dr. Everett watched him shrewdly. "I can't stop you, Harvey," he said, "or you either, Les. In some ways I don't even want to. There's a lot more at stake than myself. We all know that. But it isn't going to be pleasant for either of you to take, nor for me to watch. De Grasse is sure to get that Chair of Medicine, for one thing, and I shall always know you should have had it, Les, more now than ever before."

The hot water was still running. "A few days ago," Cyrus remarked over his shoulder, "you said that gossip couldn't do much damage to anyone unless he was vulnerable. Well, let's play it that way. What's the chair of medicine to a man like Dr. Willoughby?" He placed a clean empty bottle upside down on the porcelain and glanced at his chief. Suddenly he smiled and Willoughby smiled back. Sally, watching, wondered if any woman except possibly Dora Cutter would have been able to give anybody quite that look of completely unemotional warmth and understanding. "A natural death and an understandable suicide," said Cyrus almost casually as he dried his hands, "not a shred of evidence to the contrary." He took his eyes from Willoughby's. "There's once when you can't say I haven't followed your orders, sir," he said and moved over toward Sally. "Let's get outside, kid, and keep people out till the police arrive."

XXV

Sally stood beside Cyrus in the hall. The closed door was behind them, and behind it was the end of all their worries, but such an end. You almost wished, not almost, you did wish you'd never found the end. She looked at Cyrus. He was staring straight ahead of him. She had never felt more in need of comfort in her life, but she was perfectly aware that any comforting that was going to be passed around right now must come from her. She tried to imagine how Cyrus would be feeling, only a few yards, only a few minutes from a suicide he was responsible for. It wasn't hard to imagine, but it wasn't fun either. You had to say something to make him feel better, and anything there was to say was all wrong.

She touched his hand gently and when he didn't

264

seem to notice, drew her own back again, and, drawing it back, realized she still had that letter she had found in her desk clutched in the other hand. Open it, she thought, open it while you try to think of something to say. Maybe it'll be amusing, something to distract you both while you wait for the coroner. She shivered slightly as her mind formed the word.

It was a good thing it was Sunday, she thought inconsequentially as she worked at the tightly sealed flap. Any other day the corridors would be full of people who thought they had a right to ask questions in the name of friendship. But the only people going past so far today had been two student nurses she didn't know who had cast curious glances as they went by but nothing more, and Roberts, the pediatrics intern, who was too rushed and sleepy after a Saturday night to come out with anything more than a languid hyah and Cyrus hadn't even answered that.

Evelyn had been on the ward a little earlier relieving the medication nurse, but she had been too busy to more than smile faintly at Sally, and Sally had been too worried about what was ahead of her to more than smile back. She didn't know whether Evelyn was still on the ward or not and it didn't seem to matter. None of this really concerned Evelyn, now. It was too final, too finished for any question of justice or retribution. The only thing that concerned Evelyn was that nothing of this was ever going to come out, nothing.

She had the envelope open now. There were a couple of sheets of paper inside and inside them a second envelope. She unfolded the sheets and looked at the second envelope. Why, that was funny, Dr. Henry Bowman, but with no address or stamp. Could someone have slipped it in by mistake? Around a hospital, of course, people were always getting crank letters and Henry Bowman was on psycho. But this handwriting didn't look like a crank's. Small, a little too precise perhaps, but eminently controlled.

She opened the sheets that were around the envelope and began to read. There were only a few lines on the first sheet and she turned quickly to the second. And then she stopped worrying about whether Cyrus needed comforting or not. She was shaking his arm, pulling at his coat to bring him back from whatever dark dream world he was in.

"Cy, this is bad. We've got to do something and quick. Listen, Cy. Evelyn is running away, really away, from what she says, and she's leaving me a farewell note for Henry Bowman and listen, Cy, for heaven's sake, a confession of the murder of her mother."

He looked down at her without understanding. "But she didn't do it. She couldn't have because Kenny would never have . . ."

"Of course she didn't." Sally was impatient. "But that wouldn't stop her from confessing and it wouldn't stop this confession from bringing the whole thing out into the open if it ever got to the police. She trusts me, she says, the crazy kid, to hand it over to the police if they should arrest Dr. Everett."

Cyrus still looked uncomprehending as he took the two sheets, but when he finished reading first one, then the other, there was worry on his face. "I knew she was upset about him yesterday afternoon when he told her all those things but I never thought . . . This hospital is full of the lousiest set of loyalties I've ever run across. She must have thought she owed him this for murdering her mother to save her. Not a very logical reason, not much common sense to it either. It never would have worked, but she must have thought it would."

"She wasn't exactly brought up in an atmosphere of logic or common sense either," Sally burst out at him. "Let's not stand here and analyze her for gosh sake; let's do something."

"Well, we'll have to talk to her, I guess. Where is she?"

"I don't know. I saw her on the ward an hour or so ago. She may be gone. She put these letters in my desk thinking I wouldn't get them till tomorrow. And I might not have. It was just chance that I remembered I'd left my watch there."

"Go see if she's still there." Cyrus was maddeningly reasonable. "I'll wait here for you."

267

Sally flew down the corridor to the ward. "Have you seen Miss Moore?" She tried to make her voice matter of fact but she was panting.

"She was here awhile ago." One of the student nurses she didn't know answered. "I think she's gone off duty for the day, unless she had some other medicines to give upstairs."

"Where would she have gone upstairs?"

"Well, maybe the babies' wards." The student didn't seem to care and Sally wondered if she was going to be able to keep from screaming, because if Evelyn was gone how could they find her, how could they ever find her?

"She might still be in the drug closet." This came casually from the other student who was passing.

Sally didn't even thank her, just hurried off to where such a short time ago she had seen Miss Kenny take three tablets out of the wrong bottle. She looked in. Empty.

"They said she might be up in the babies' ward," she panted as she went by Cyrus, and felt brief anger as he nodded almost absently. Didn't he realize how dreadful this could be, Evelyn going off doing something perhaps desperate, and all so unnecessarily. You could send out searchers. You could put personals in the papers, but she might never be found, might never look at a paper.

"She left just a few minutes ago. She said she was

through for the day. I was glad because she looked tired." This was the nurse upstairs. Perhaps she could catch her in her room, but better tell Cy first. There was a dull ache inside her as she went down the stairs again and toward the nurses' office. And then the ache leaped into a sharp pain for a second and then stopped, for Cy was standing there lounging against the door and in front of him, her back to the hall was a small slim figure in blue. "Evelyn," she started to call, but Cy had cast her a quick warning glance and motioned with one hand down by his side, and *shut up,* she realized afterwards, had never been said more silently or more loudly.

She could hear him talking as she came up behind, the girl. It wasn't Cyrus' way to sound dispassionate, and she wondered as she listened what the measured words were costing him in repressions.

"Glad you happened along, Miss Moore. Looks as if I owe you an apology. Looks as if I owe a number of people an apology as a matter of fact. That thing we were talking about yesterday at lunch and later with Dr. Everett, that business about your aunt's death not being natural. Well, we've gone into it pretty thoroughly since then and it looks as if I was all wrong. It looks as if your aunt really did die of insulin fastness," the words came with slow deliberation, "and all that other stuff I was stewing about was just the bunk."

Sally could see the girl's shoulder twitch to attention, her body stiffen in disbelief. "But those insulin bottles you said were changed," she protested breathlessly. "Miss Pepper being pushed under the car . . ."

Cyrus shrugged. "There may have been something wrong with one of the bottles of insulin. That's what got me off on the wrong track and from there I guess I just went haywire. As for Sally being pushed, we looked where it happened and someone had dropped a jar of ointment. The walk was slippery and probably she went so fast she thought she was being pushed."

"It doesn't make sense," said Evelyn slowly. "I don't believe it. It couldn't all be so different."

"Couldn't it?" Cyrus shrugged again. "Well, that's the only way I know to explain it now. If it doesn't satisfy you, kid, you'd better go higher up. Ask Dr. Everett, why don't you? But don't bother him for a day or so. He's got his hands pretty full." He nodded gravely toward the locked door behind him. "Damn shame. Miss Kenny—suicide. Grief for your aunt, everyone seems to think. Dr. Everett's in there now."

The girl turned from Cyrus with a bewildered look on her face, and saw Sally and saw the letters in her hand, and her face went white. "Oh," she said, and put her hand up to her cheek abruptly. "I didn't think you'd . . ."

"I just happened to go to my desk." Sally smiled

270

and held them toward her. "I'm sorry—no I'm not. It's nice to know what people will do for other people, but you won't want me to keep them now, will you?"

"No." Evelyn sounded almost as if she were sleep walking. She stood there looking at the letters in her hand as if she didn't see them.

"Want a match?" Cyrus drawled the words and held out a bent paper packet. "There's a hell of a big ash tray in there." He nodded toward the doctor's office across the hall.

Sally looked at him and nodded. She and Evelyn disappeared into the doctor's room. When they came out they both were smiling. "I'll phone the Infirmary," Sally was saying, "and tell Miss Markham to give you the keys. The car's right out in the parking place. You and Henry Bowman drive out and see your aunt. Sure he can get off for a couple of hours if it's important. His patients aren't sick. They're just crazy."

Evelyn looked at them both and suddenly her eyes were full of tears. "I can't remember when I've been able to cry before," she said wonderingly. "I suppose I ought to thank you for that along—along with all the rest."

They watched her blue and white skirt swish slowly around the corner. Sally shook her head wearily. "Every baby, Cy," she said, "always seems to end up in your lap. Nice for the babies but tough for you."

"I wasn't exactly looking for a dress rehearsal, right now." Cyrus grinned, but his grin was weary too. "I was staring out into the hall thinking how lousy the whole thing was and wondering where you'd find the kid, if at all. Then along scurries a little blue nurse and it's Evelyn and that kind of puts it up to me. Lucky to have had it, though, probably. If it went over with her it'll go over a lot easier with the boys. They don't know so much. And as far as we're concerned, from now on nobody is going to know anything."

"Dora Cutter will have to know."

"Yes," he noded absently, "but she's good at keeping things to herself."

"Yes," agreed Sally, thinking how much truer that was than Cyrus knew. Then because she couldn't help it, she said, "Anyway, she won't think you're a crack pot. Aren't you glad of that?"

"Glad?" Cyrus looked down at her curiously and considered the question. "Well, yes, I've a lot of respect for that mind of hers."

"How about mine?" Sally could have choked, but the words came out in spite of herself. Her face was burning but they were out.

Cyrus was still looking down at her. His tired face lighted up a little. "Respect is hardly the word, kid,

272

neither as a matter of fact is mind. I'll tell you about it some time when I feel better."

"I can hardly wait." Sally's light touch returned, as always with confidence, but not for long. "I can't stand it, Cy," she exploded, "the idea of this whole dumb hospital going around saying you're an addle-pated sensation monger. They're going to, of course, and it's not fair for you to have to take all that when you've been so—so stupendous."

"Fair?" Cyrus voice was scathing but not of her. "Sure it's fair, and then some. Because, look, who the hell am I to think I have to know everything, to go round playing God? If Kenny was guilty for doing something she thought had to be done, if Willoughby was guilty, subconsciously or not, for letting her get away with it, what about me? Do you realize, kid, that if I hadn't been so damn curious in the very be-ginning everything would be just the way it is now, except we all would have missed these last few happy days—and Kenny wouldn't be dead. Why should she be dead? It's all very well to talk about justice, but who am I to administer it? The government takes care of that, and if this was too big for the govern-ment it was too big for me. Willoughby saw that. He tried to make me see it too. Everybody tried to make me see it, as a matter of fact. But I was too smart. Nope, Sal, I don't feel so good about my handling of this fine little affair. If you want to know, I feel lousy.

If I've got a lot to take, well, I've got it coming to me." He grinned and it was pretty close to a humble grin. "It won't hurt me either."

She looked at him and touched his hand again. "No," she said softly, "it won't hurt you."